Royal Kitchen Restaurant

Introduction:

Bai Xiangning, the royal chef, unfortunately fell off a cliff while searching for rare ingredients. When he opened his eyes again, he found that he had entered a whole new world.The royal chef who had a high status in his previous life turned into a pauper heavily in debt.In order to change the predicament, Bai Xiangning opened a small restaurant by using her unparalleled cooking skills.Did you hear that there's a new little restaurant on the corner of the streetWhy is it located in such a remote location that no one would go there If you open a small restaurant, you will definitely lose all your money.Everyone is waiting to see Bai Xiangning's joke.Bai Xiangning didn't care what the outside world said. She was shaking the spatula and concentrating on studying the sauce needed for the new dish.Later, everyone who ate at Bai's Little Restaurant was so delicious.Woohoo, it's so delicious. There is such a delicious claypot rice in the world. What I ate before was all rubbish.Boss Bai, give me another sour plum soup. He said this while raising the twenty-liter mineral water bucket in his hand.The sweet and sour pork ribs are sold out and won't be available until tomorrow. So I won't leave. I'll wait here until tomorrow. I must be the first one to eat it.The new dishes in the small restaurant are the same, such as mapo tofu, dry pot sausage, plum ribs, lamb chop pilaf, and tomato and potato beef brisket. There is nothing that customers can't imagine, and there is nothing they can't eat.The diners were obsessed with Boss Bai's cooking skills and couldn't help themselves. Just as they were immersed in eating, they were surprised to find that more and more people were queuing up in Bai's small restaurant, and there were even many famous and familiar faces.shockEven the heir to Chaoxu Group, the largest company in Jinghua City, showed up at the small restaurantBai's Little Restaurant grew in size, with branches all over the city, and eventually became the famous Xiang Ning Restaurant.

Chapter 1In the early summer evening, the heat of the day gradually dissipates as the sun sets, and it becomes cooler.Behind No. 17 Middle School is a long snack street, which sells pancakes, rice bowls, fried skewers, self-service hotpots, and everything else.Students who had just finished school poured out of the campus in droves. Their only destination was the snack street.After entering the snack street, they ran towards different stores. Before long, every store was full of people.There are not only schools next to the snack street, but also several office buildings and residential buildings. Many people come to eat, so the snack street is very lively every day.Walking straight along this street, just around the corner, there are two stores that continue to do their job, one is a hardware store, and the other sells general merchandise.It is completely different from the previous scene. It seems to be isolated in a separate space and no one cares about it.Old lady, did you knock on the door today and there was still no movementThe person who spoke was Uncle Chen, the owner of the hardware store. They opened this store together as an old couple. They were here when the snack street was still in its infancy. They probably opened it for more than ten years.In the past two days, I knocked on the door whenever I had time, and even leaned at the door and listened carefully, but it was quiet inside, without a sound. The old lady looked worried and sighed several times. Do you think anything will happen to this child after he has locked himself in the house for so many daysSuch a big change happened in the family, and the child Xiang Ning must have been hit hard. Her body has been weak since she was a child. How can she endure these two days without eating or drinkingThe department store next to the hardware store was opened by Bai Xiangning's parents and had been on this street for almost ten years. The two families had always had a good relationship. Uncle Chen and his wife regarded Bai Xiangning as their granddaughter.A few days ago, Bai Xiangning's parents had a car accident while they were shopping for goods. The place they went to was in a mountainous area. It was remote and the road was narrow. The car rolled over without knowing what happened.When it was found, the car was completely destroyed and the people inside were missing.At first, Bai Xiangning held on to hope and insisted on looking for them. After all, as long as the bodies were not found, there was still a possibility of living.But after half a month of searching, there was still no trace of them.When the police finally told Bai Xiangning the news and told her that her parents had almost no chance of survival, she immediately fainted.After waking up, I locked myself in the store owned by my parents and didn't come out for two or three days.How about I knock on the door again If there's still no movement inside, then we'll call the police.Uncle Chen walked back and forth, but in the end he felt uneasy, worried that something might happen to Bai Xiangning inside, so he walked to the door of the department store and knocked hard.A splitting headache.Bai Xiangning's head seemed to have been hit hard by a heavy object. The pain was unbearable, but she was dragged by the nightmare and could not wake up for a long time.She remembered that she had just picked a rare fungus on the cliff, which only appeared after it rained.She was only focused on reaching for the rare bacteria on the edge of the cliff, but she forgot that the ground was slippery after the rain. She accidentally stepped on the ground and fell straight down the cliff.During the fall, her head hit a jumble of rocks, and then she lost all consciousness.Boom, boom, boom.When Bai Xiangning was unconscious, she seemed to hear someone knocking on the door.But she clearly fell off the cliff. It stands to reason that she should be passed out in a wilderness somewhere. How could she hear the knock on the doordong dong dongThe sound got louder and louder, and the person knocking on the door seemed very anxious.Bai Xiangning struggled for a long time and finally regained her consciousness. She slowly opened her eyes and woke up.She found that she had been lying on the cold ground.The moment she woke up, all the memories rushed into her mind instantly, and the impact of a large amount of information almost made her faint again.She pressed her temples and struggled to understand her situation.She should have died when she fell from the cliff, but she was not completely dead. Now her soul has been transferred to another person's body.This is a brand new world, completely different from her original one.Bai Xiangning stretched out her hand to hold the chair next to her, trying to stand up.There was a clang.Her legs softened and she knelt down directly on the ground.My body has no strength at all, and I feel weak all over.Bai Xiangning was horrified. There wouldn't be anything wrong with her current body, rightBai Xiangning felt relieved when she felt a sharp pain in her stomach.It seemed like he was just hungry.Just cook a meal to fill your stomach.She was an imperial chef in her previous life, so cooking is a piece of cake for her.Bai Xiangning tried to stand up again, but almost fell to her knees again. Now it was difficult for her to even stand up. How could she still have the strength to cook by herselfSo there was only one thought left in her mindShe is really starving to death. Can you give her something to eat to keep her aliveThe knocking on the door downstairs continued.Bai Xiangning first held on to the handle of the chair, then held on to the wall, using all the tools she could hold on to, staggering downstairs, and finally reached the door with great difficulty.Facing the closed door, she searched in the memory of the original owner for a long time before she found the location of the key.Uncle Chen kept knocking on the door for a long time. He originally planned to call the police, but when he got closer, he heard a slight sound of walking coming from inside.His heart dropped. The child Xiang Ning should be fine.He waited patiently outside for a while.Two minutes later, the locked door opened from the inside, and Bai Xiangning walked out into the dusk.Seeing that she was safe and sound, Uncle Chen finally felt relieved.But the next second.Because this body had not eaten for several days, and because she had just gone downstairs and exhausted her last bit of strength, Bai Xiangning fainted again.Uncle Chen was startled, and with agility that was not suitable for his age, he supported Bai Xiangning to prevent her from falling flat on her back.He called his wife, and together they helped Bai Xiangning to the recliner. The old lady was worried and took out her mobile phone to call an ambulance, but was stopped by Uncle Chen.Xiang Ning's child is probably fine. He probably fainted from hunger.How do you know what to do if she gets sickUncle Chen said: Just before she fainted, I heard her stomach growl loudly.When Bai Xiangning woke up, the sky had completely darkened. When she lowered her head and looked down, she found that she was lying on a recliner with a thin blanket wrapped around her.Oh, Xiang Ning, you kid finally woke up.The old lady walked over with a face of surprise and held Bai Xiangning's hand.Bai Xiangning reacted for a moment and recognized the old man in front of her. She knew that the old man was really worried about her, so she gave a reassuring smile, "Grandma Chen, don't worry, I'm fine."I cooked some porridge at night and took it out of the pot in advance. Now it is not so hot. Grandma Chen handed her the bowl, "Eat quickly, you must be starving after not eating for so long."Bai Xiangning was so hungry that she ate three large bowls of porridge with pickles. After eating, her stomach, which had been battered by not eating for a long time, was relieved and she felt much better.There is still something in the pot, do you want more Uncle Chen asked with concern. He had a spoon in his hand and seemed to be preparing to fill another bowl for Bai Xiangning.Bai Xiangning felt a little embarrassed, Grandpa Chen, I'm full, thank you.Thank you for letting her eat hot porridge when she was about to starve to death after she came to this strange world.Oh, why are you so polite to us We are all relieved to see that you are fine.After eating, Bai Xiangning recovered a lot of strength and helped clear away the dishes on the table. She originally wanted to wash the dishes, but Grandma Chen said that what she needed most now was to get enough rest. I really couldn't resist it, so I had no choice but to give up.After having a full meal and resting for a while, Bai Xiangning was able to think about her next plan.Her parents used to run a department store. Now that they have passed away, how to run the department store has become a problem that Bai Xiangning urgently needs to solve.Bai Xiangning knew almost nothing about purchasing channels, product prices, and department store varieties. Her parents' accident happened so suddenly that there was no way she could tell her anything in advance.After much thought, Bai Xiangning decided to transform the department store into a small restaurant.She had two thoughts.On this street that mainly sells snacks, the survival of department stores has become increasingly difficult. Although my parents have been sticking to the store and tried many ways, the business is still declining day by day.For a long time, department stores have been in a state of loss. If this continues, it will be a matter of time before they go bankrupt.In addition, Bai Xiangning was the youngest and most talented royal chef in the palace in her previous life, and her cooking skills were her most reliable and proudest skill.Although she is now in a brand new world, she firmly believes that as long as her craftsmanship is there, she can make a difference no matter what era she is in.After she decided to open a small restaurant, a ding rang in her head.Congratulations to the host for finding his goal. As the host's right-hand man, I will do my best to help the host fulfill his wish.

who is talkingThe system explained a lot to her. After listening to it, Bai Xiangning understood, so you are a tool that can help me fulfill my wish.system:Yes, I am an emotionless tool:Bai Xiangning was a little curious about how the system would help her, but the system only said it mysteriously. She would naturally know it after the host opened the restaurant.Too many things happened on this day. Not only did she come to a new world, she even had a magical system that claimed to help her realize her wishes.At night, she fell into a deep sleep almost as soon as her head hit the pillow.After a night's rest, Bai Xiangning's energy recovered to 100%.So early the next morning, she went to the largest vegetable market nearby, planning to buy some vegetables to take back and cook.Uncle Chen and his wife got up and found that Bai Xiangning was missing. Their hearts were hanging again and they quickly called Bai Xiangning.Jingle BellBai Xiangning just walked in with her bag, and the old couple breathed a sigh of relief when they saw her.Grandpa Chen, Grandma Chen, I went to the vegetable market to buy some food, and I cooked for lunch. She lifted the bag in her hand, and inside was a snakehead fish weighing more than two kilograms. It was jumping around so much that the inside of the bag was splashed with water stains.The old couple looked at each other. It turned out that Xiang Ning had gone to the vegetable market. She just said that she was cooking for lunch. I had never heard that this child could cook. Could she be bluffing themLet me cook at noon. Grandma Chen took the bag from Bai Xiangning's hand. The black fish inside flicked violently, and the bag was torn with a loud bang. She was startled and almost threw the fish and bag together.Grandma Chen was worried that she had never cooked snakehead, a fish with a fierce nature, and this really stumped her.Seeing this, Bai Xiangning carried the bag to the kitchen, then took the fish out of the bag and put it into the pool.Grandma Chen, let me borrow the kitchen. She poked her head out and said to Old Mrs. Chen who was standing outside.The old couple looked curiously into the kitchen, and saw Bai Xiangning raising the knife and striking the black fish hard on the head with the back of the knife in a very calm manner. The black fish that had been struggling suddenly stopped moving.Before the old couple could be surprised, Bai Xiangning turned the knife over and made a quick and precise cut on the fish belly, making the incision neatly. She pulled out the internal organs of the black fish in three strokes, and scraped off the mucus on the surface of the black fish with the tip of a knife, and the whole black fish was ready.Uncle Chen and his wife were amazed. Bai Xiangning's technique looked like she had practiced it before, and she didn't look like a novice at all, so they stopped worrying about it and left the kitchen completely to Bai Xiangning.After Bai Xiangning heated the pot to 70% heat, fry the fish pieces and fish bones for one minute. When the fish bones become brown, add enough boiling water, then add a small amount of ginger slices, continue to cook over high heat, and then As time goes by, the soup in the pot boils and gradually becomes thicker and whiter, and the fragrance of the fish soup spreads.Uncle Chen, who was sitting outside reading the newspaper, followed the unusual smell and walked to the kitchen.Xiang Ning, what are you cooking Why does it smell so good

chapter 2I'm cooking one fish and two meals. Grandpa Chen, please wait a moment. I'll make it right away.Bai Xiangning was not idle while the soup was stewing. She slurried the prepared fish fillets and prepared some green and red peppers as side dishes. The black fish fillets were firm and not as fragile as other fish. So she couldn't help stir-frying, so she quickly stirred the pot a few times, stir-fried evenly, and put the fish fillets on the plate.The wife next to him teased him in a low voice: Are you greedyNo rush, no rush, I'm not hungry at all. Uncle Chen raised his voice and said to Bai Xiangning.He sat back on the recliner, refusing to admit that he was greedy.My wife laughed and said: I didn't expect Xiang Ning to actually know how to cook, and the smell is just good. Don't tell me, I'm a little curious about what the food she cooks tastes like.Soon, Bai Xiangning's fish and two dishes were on the table.The so-called one-fish-two-eat method is to stew the fish bones in soup, while the fish fillets are used to stir-fry.After stir-frying at high temperature, the fish fillets become slightly curled. The white fish fillets are covered with a thin layer of paste, which is shiny and oily. The side dishes are rich in color, and the whole dish is full of color and fragrance.She served two bowls of milky white fish soup to the old couple.The key to making the fish soup thick and white is to fry the fish bones thoroughly, and then pour boiling water into it and cook it over high heat.Uncle Chen couldn't wait any longer. He blew it twice hastily and took a big sip of fish soup without caring about burning it.The high-temperature frying takes away the fishy smell of the fish bones. Even though there are not many seasonings in the fish soup, just ginger slices and salt, it is still mellow and delicious, sliding across the throat like silk, bringing relief to the stomach.Grandma Chen picked up a piece of fish. The fried fish fillet only used the simplest seasoning, but it brought out the deliciousness of the black fish to the extreme.She didn't really like eating fish because she always got thorns stuck in her throat.However, the black fish has less bones and firm meat. It becomes extremely smooth and tender after being coated in the gravy. The addition of green and red peppers, green onions and ginger gives the fish fillets a different aroma. The whole dish is very harmonious.Both dishes have a light taste, which is very suitable for elderly people like them. After a meal, their stomachs will feel so comfortable.Grandma Chen praised: Xiang Ning, your craftsmanship is really amazing. This is the best fish soup I have ever tasted.Grandpa Chen also gave her a thumbs up.After dinner, Bai Xiangning told them about her plans.When they heard that Bai Xiangning was going to change her family's department store into a restaurant, they were all a little surprised.This street is full of snack shops. Moreover, the location here is not good and too remote. If you open a restaurant, you may not be able to compete with others. The issues that Uncle Chen considered were very realistic, and they were ones that Bai Xiangning had thought about before.Grandma Chen held Bai Xiangning's hand and said: "Although what Grandpa Chen said makes sense, we can't make decisions for you. If you really think about it, then feel free to do it boldly."Grandpa Chen was worried that Bai Xiangning would be hit by what he just said, so he also said: Your craftsmanship is so good, if you open a restaurant, you can definitely make a career. We are older and our thinking cannot keep up with your young people, but if you need our help, just ask.Bai Xiangning's nose felt sore after hearing this.In her previous life, she was an orphan and had never felt the warmth of family affection. I learned the news of the death of my parents just after I came back to this life. I thought I would go back to the time when I was alone again, but I didn't expect that I would experience the rare family affection from my neighbor's grandparents.They really treated her like their own granddaughter.Before Bai Xiangning could say anything, a burst of noise suddenly came from outside.Look for me inside and outsideBai Xiangning heard the sound and walked out, only to see a dark-skinned man wearing a vest standing at the door of her department store and yelling.Behind him were two arrogant men.who are youBai Xiangning asked with a frown. The leading man looked familiar, but she didn't remember who he was.You, why are you That man was stunned for a moment when he saw her, as if he wanted to say why she was here.This is my home, who are you and what are you doing hereAt first sight, these people came with bad intentions. Bai Xiangning stood in front of Grandpa Chen and Grandma Chen, questioning these people sternly.I am your uncle. The leading man suddenly gained momentum and raised his voice several decibels. You Bai Xiangning, you don't even recognize your own uncle, rightBai Xiangning stared at the man's face for a long time. She remembered that she did have an uncle, but she hadn't seen him for many years.In the memory of the original owner, this uncle loved gambling, and the family used to be harmonious. Later, because of his gambling addiction, the family house was ruined, and his wife divorced him with their children.Later, he still did not repent and kept borrowing money to gamble.Although he never showed up at Bai's house during holidays, he always contacted his sister, Bai Xiangning's mother, to ask for money to gamble.First, he made excuses about investing, and then he said he had been defrauded of money. In short, he lied all the time.Bai Xiangning's mother believed in him at first and was willing to lend him money, but later she recognized his true face and refused to give him a penny no matter how much he pestered her.The original owner was extremely disgusted with this uncle. Because of his existence, his parents had quarreled countless times.Under Bai Xiangning's scrutinizing gaze, Ding Chou felt guilty for no reason.But he straightened up immediately. He had a legitimate reason for coming today. How could he be so timid in front of a little girlRemember who I amBai Xiangning didn't answer, but asked him instead.Ding Chou took two steps forward, pointed to the department store behind him and said, "I'll get what belongs to me."Bai Xiangning's face darkened.She knew that this uncle had no good intentions. After not showing up for so long, the sudden appearance turned out to be the idea of a department store.The department store is opened by my parents, what does it have to do with youWhy does it have nothing to do with me I am your uncle. Your parents are dead and you are a little girl who doesn't know how to open a store. Of course, I should run this store.What he said was completely untenable, but he said it as a matter of course, as if he was saying something particularly reasonable.Before Bai Xiangning could answer, he continued: Your parents must have told you where the house book is. Stop inking and give me the house book quickly. I will go through the transfer tomorrow. When uncle takes over the department store and starts the business, you will definitely be able to make a living.You are too thick-skinned, right Uncle Chen, who was standing behind, had heard about Uncle Bai Xiangning's bad deeds. He really couldn't bear to listen and said: Even if Xiangning's parents died, this shop should still be fragrant. Ning inheritance, what does it have to do with youThis dead old man came out of nowhere. This is our family matter. It's not your turn as an outsider to interfere. Ding Chou's tone was so arrogant that it made people want to beat him up.Bai Xiangning glared at him: There is no house book here. If you make trouble again, I will call the police.Ding Chou just thought she was scaring him and yelled: How is it possible that I heard your mother say before that the house book is in an old box with a copper lock Go and find it for me.Bai Xiangning took out her mobile phone and wanted to call the police.Seeing that she was serious, Ding Chou quickly stepped forward and tried to stop her. Hey, hey, hey, if you have something to say, please say it. Don't call the police.Bai Xiangning didn't say a word, and her cold eyes made Ding Chou feel a flinch. He wanted to say something more, but in front of Bai Xiangning, he found that he couldn't say a word.She is obviously just a little girl in her early twenties, how could she have such a terrifying auraDing Chou originally thought that Bai Xiangning would be easy to handle after losing her parents, but she didn't expect it to be so difficult.He led people out of the department store with a stern look on his face.Bai Xiangning kept staring at his back until he walked out of the snack street.Xiang Ning, will your uncle come to make trouble again Now that your parents are not here, we are both old bones. What will happen if he comes againGrandma Chen said worriedly.Don't worry, even if he comes again, I have a way to deal with it.At night, Bai Xiangning found the old box Ding Chou mentioned in the bedroom on the second floor. After opening it, there was indeed a department store house book on the top.After she picked up the house book, she found that underneath was a thick envelope with some yellowing edges.The cover is written in beautiful handwriting: a dowry saved for my precious daughter.Bai Xiangning held the thick envelope and didn't dare to open it for a moment.She took a deep breath and slowly opened the envelope. Inside was a neat stack of hundred-dollar bills, estimated to be tens of thousands of dollars.Bai Xiangning's eyes were red. Although her parents were gone when she came into this world, their love silently surrounded her.Whether it was this department store or the money they left her, it made it easier for her to survive in this strange world.She placed the house book in another safe and airtight place, and then said silently in her heart: No matter what, she will guard this store and will not let anyone take it away.Bai Xiangning is a man of action.

When she said she was going to open a store, she started without delay.She disposed of all the remaining department stores in the store at cost prices. If she couldn't dispose of them, she returned them to the manufacturers.The next step was to decorate the store, but finding a decorator gave her a hard time.The decoration industry is too deep, and with the current funds in her hands, it is difficult to find a reliable decoration team.Knowing her troubles, Uncle Chen patted his thigh and said, "Isn't this a coincidence My son is a decorator and he did all the decoration in your store."Uncle Chen's son came over with a few people the next day, and their price was much lower than the market price Bai Xiangning had inquired about. Originally, she wanted to raise more money to pay more, but both Uncle Chen and his son said No need, it's just a matter of effort for the neighbors.Bai Xiangning can only use what she is best at to repay them.The next day she got up early and went to the vegetable market to buy vegetables, and just in time the butcher shop owner brought in a batch of pork belly.Seeing her passing by, the boss greeted her warmly: Girl, come and take a look at my pork. The black pork I just slaughtered this morning is very fresh.The pork belly has distinct layers, the lean meat is delicate, and the fat part even shows a translucent texture under the light. At first glance, it looks like home-raised local pork.Bai Xiangning pointed to a piece of pork belly and said: "Give me this piece."The boss quickly cut the meat for her and said with a smile: This is the best piece of meat. The girl has really good eyesight.Bai Xiangning smiled, picked up the bag of pork belly, and went to buy some vegetables.She plans to make fried noodles for lunch.She first cut the pork belly into small pieces of about one centimeter, then put it into the pot and slowly stir-fried it. After the oil came out, she added the chopped green onion and ginger to remove the fishy smell and add fragrance to the meat. When the pork belly After most of the fat has come out, pour the Bai Xiang Ning into the sauce and start to simmer over low heat.When making fried noodles, sauce is extremely important. Soybean sauce, sweet noodle sauce and dry yellow sauce are indispensable. Simmer slowly for about an hour, until all the flavors of the sauce are blended together, and the sauce is ready.When the sauce was almost ready, Bai Xiangning started cooking the noodles. She used hand-rolled noodles. This kind of noodles was smooth and chewy, making it the best choice for making fried noodles with soybean paste.Have you ever smelled a strong smell of meatChen Feng suddenly asked.The others also stopped what they were doing, sniffed in unison, and then showed intoxicated expressions. It smells so good. I heard that the little girl from the Bai family is very skilled at her young age. She must be making delicious food.At this time, Uncle Chen came over and said, "Let's rest for a while. It's time to have lunch."Everyone washed their hands and then walked to the nearby hardware store. Since the department store was under renovation, Bai Xiangning borrowed the kitchen of Uncle Chen's house and ate at his house.As they got closer, the smell of meat became stronger and stronger.Several people's stomachs growled in unison.Bai Xiangning opened the kitchen door, and the smell of fried sauce was as impactful as a beast emerging from its cage.I made fried noodles for lunch, come and eat.Bai Xiangning greeted warmly.

Chapter 3The kitchen door was fully open, and from Chen Feng's angle, he could just see the fried sauce that Bai Xiangning had just poured out.That's where the rich aroma comes from.Bai Xiangning boiled a lot of fried sauce and put it in a very large stainless steel basin.A thin layer of clear oil floats on top of the fried sauce, while the diced pork belly is wrapped in dark brown sauce and sinks to the bottom of the basin.The noodles used for fried sauce must be cooked and eaten right away. Bai Xiangning took the steaming noodles out of the pot and quickly ran them through cold water to make them smooth and elastic.She took several large noodle bowls to serve noodles for everyone, and poured a large spoonful of fried sauce on the noodles. Finally, she added some cucumber shreds and vegetable shreds.Chen Feng took it and picked up the noodles with chopsticks. The sauce on the top immediately flowed slowly down the noodles. He stirred it a few more times with chopsticks so that every noodle was evenly coated with fried sauce and shiny. bright. Thinly chopped cucumbers are mixed in, and the brown-red noodles with soy sauce have a hint of green color.This fried noodles looks so appetizing, rightChen Feng couldn't restrain himself anymore, picked up a chopstick and put it into his mouth. The noodles were smooth and chewy, and very chewy.The diced pork belly has been stir-fried, and the edges are caramelized. The meat is full of juice when you chew it. The excess fat of the meat has been refined, so it doesn't taste greasy at all. Take a light bite and the fat will melt in your mouth immediately, making you slim. The tenderness of the meat and the oily aroma of the fat blend together in your mouth, and the more you eat, the more delicious it becomes.Chen Feng had never eaten fried noodles before. In the past, he often bought fried noodles at roadside stalls for ten yuan a portion, but the sauce was not thick, the meat had no flavor, and the noodles were mushy. lump.Later, he also ate at some well-known time-honored restaurants, but among the many restaurants he had eaten at, none of them served noodles as delicious as they do today.He ate the noodles with big mouthfuls, and soon the bowl was empty.He held the bowl and looked at Bai Xiangning.PoofMrs. Chen laughed out loud. Chen Feng turned his head and found several empty bowls being lifted up next to him.His colleague, like him, ate a bowl of fried noodles and was still not full."Help me serve some more," a colleague said first, passing the bowl to Bai Xiangning.Just as Bai Xiangning was about to reach out to take it, the bowl in front of her was pushed back by another pair of hands. She served it to me first and I finished it first.Several people were grabbing it, and Bai Xiangning didn't know whether to laugh or cry, so she could only say: "Don't worry, there is a lot of fried sauce left, I will serve it to you now."While others were still waiting, Chen Feng had already walked out of the kitchen with a bowl full of noodles.Why did you secretly serve so much fried noodles behind our backs The others began to attack Chen Feng.Chen Feng said proudly: "What do you know This means making enough food and clothing by yourself."He no longer paid attention to the others and just held the bowl of noodles and inhaled the storm.Bai Xiangning acted very quickly, and the others didn't wait long before eating the hot fried noodles.Although Chen Feng had just eaten a bowl, it only put a shallow layer in his stomach, which was far from full.He wanted to be more reserved, but the delicious food in front of himThe aroma of fried sauce and the meaty aroma of diced pork belly kept attacking his psychological defense line, making him unable to control himself at all.He quickly mixed the noodles and put it into his mouth. The noodles are distinct and each one is covered in thick sauce, and the cucumber shreds as a side dish bring a fresh taste to this bowl of noodles.When he was about to finish eating, Chen Feng rolled up the last few noodles and dipped all the remaining sauce in the bowl without leaving any behind.When he finished the last bite, he couldn't help but let out a long sigh.This was the most satisfying and delicious meal he had ever had.It was a bit hot in the store at noon. Uncle Chen and his wife have always been very frugal and did not install air conditioning in the store, so everyone was sweating profusely after eating.Bai Xiangning moved a large electric fan and turned it on so that everyone could get some wind.She thought for a while and went to the canteen outside to buy a few bottles of ice-cold soda.When Chen Feng and others took the soda, a chill spread directly to the whole body along the fingertips, and the heat just now was reduced a lot.Sister Xiang Ning, you are so thoughtful.Bai Xiangning smiled and said: It should be.People came all the way to help. She couldn't accept other people's kindness in vain. She had to do something within her ability.Although they were neighbors, they actually had no obligation to help her like this. She couldn't take other people's kindness for granted.Since Bai Xiangning's store used to sell groceries, almost all of the store had to be renovated, including laying the floor, building counters, adding tables and chairs, and customizing the door. It took more than two weeks to basically complete it.She was not idle while the store was being renovated. She made several trips to get the business license and other documents needed to open a restaurant.The second floor had been used as the living room before. It used to be fine for their family of three, but now she is alone, and it is a waste to live in such a big house.She originally wanted to decorate the second floor into private rooms, but just the decoration on the first floor cost almost all her money.Bai Xiangning stood at the stairs leading to the second floor, thinking that she should wait until later to talk about the second floor. Now her small restaurant is still in its infancy, and the venue on the first floor is enough. When the number of guests increases later, she Then decorate the second floor.After the decoration of the first floor was completed, Bai Xiangning cooked the food herself and invited Uncle Chen's family of three and several other members of the decoration team to have a meal together.This time, Bai Xiangning started preparing the ingredients a day in advance and cooked ten dishes that day, which could barely fit on the dining table at Uncle Chen's house.They let out an exclamation with each bite. The fried noodles made by Bai Xiangning were enough to amaze them before, but after eating the main dish she cooked, they discovered that Bai Xiangning's craftsmanship was much higher than they originally thought.Every dish has both color and flavor, and it looks like a restaurant's signature dish when taken out.Uh-huh, this braised pork is so delicious that I couldn't help but slurred with my mouth full.This fish is so delicious, how can you make it taste like thisOld man, you should eat more vegetables. You have high blood fat, so you need to eat less meat.Uncle Chen was reluctant. Although Xiang Ning was good at cooking, there was no way he could cook vegetables that tasted better than meat. How could he eat vegetables if he didn't eat the meatBut under the pressure from his wife's eyes, Uncle Chen still slowly picked up a chopstick of vegetables.As soon as he took it into his mouth, his eyes widened in surprise.This vegetable is not bland at all. There is a thin layer of lard hanging on the vegetable leaves, which brings a meaty taste to the mouth. After chewing it twice, you can taste the unique sweetness of green vegetables.Before he could speak, Uncle Chen picked up a few more vegetables with chopsticks. After a while, he, who never liked vegetables, actually ate less than half of the plate.I never thought that baby greens could be so deliciousIt seemed that it wasn't that he didn't like vegetables before, but that he had never eaten delicious stir-fried vegetables. If he is still at this level today, I can let him eat vegetables every time in the future.At first, Chen Feng and others thought that fried noodles were the ultimate delicacy, but after eating today's meal, they realized that the fried noodles before were just appetizers.Bai Xiangning's real level is far beyond their imagination.At first, when his father asked him to come over to help decorate the Bai family's department store, he was actually not optimistic about Bai Xiangning opening a restaurant, but now he hopes that Bai Xiangning will open the restaurant soon so that he can come here often in the future. time to eatDuring the renovation of the store, Bai Xiangning had already decided that the small restaurant would sell rice bowls from the beginning. It is close to the school and there are some residential areas around it. Opposite the school is an office building with dozens of floors and there are many office workers. Rice bowl is the most convenient and suitable food for these people.The most important thing is that she is only one person now and does not have enough manpower, so she naturally has to start simple.At first she planned to sell dinner first. Early in the morning, she went to the vegetable market to buy a lot of ingredients, and then started to prepare the food in the kitchen.She bought some pieces of tofu.There are different types of tofu. Nan tofu is solidified with gypsum. It has a white color and a delicate and tender texture. Northern tofu is solidified with brine, and its texture is firmer than southern tofu. It is yellow in color and older, so it is also called old tofu.The dish Bai Xiangning planned to cook required the use of southern tofu. She put the tofu she bought into clean water to maintain the delicate texture of the tofu.Since it was the first day, Bai Xiangning did not prepare a lot of ingredients. After working for about an hour, the processing of the ingredients was basically completed.After putting the processed ingredients aside into categories, Bai Xiangning turned on the fire and officially started making dinner.At five o'clock in the evening, Bai Xiangning hung a small sign at the door saying "Open".Bai's small restaurant officially opened.

Chapter 4I'm working overtime tonight and will come back late. Please make something for Tongtong to eat. He Kang'an received a call from his wife as soon as he got off work, asking him to cook for his son. He seemed worried, and his wife warned him again, "Don't buy food for Tongtong outside. The food outside is unhygienic."He Kang'an responded: Okay, okay, I understand, I will go back and cook for the child now.The wife then hung up the phone with confidence.He Kang'an was not in a hurry to go back. His son had not finished school yet, so he would find something to eat first.Every day on his way to get off work, he would pass by a snack street, which was very busy and had all kinds of snacks. He Kang'an often came here to eat, and occasionally brought his son here, of course, without his wife's knowledge.Although there are many kinds of snacks, he gets a little tired of eating them often. He wandered around for a long time without seeing anything he particularly wanted to eat. Just as he was about to leave, an unusual and spicy aroma suddenly drifted into his nose.this taste isHe followed the scent all the way to the corner of the snack street. He looked up and found that the grocery store that had been opened here had turned into a restaurant at some point.Bai's small restaurant.The name of this hotel is as inconspicuous as its location.But the alluring fragrance came from inside, and now that it was closer, the smell became stronger.Sir, what would you like to eatHe Kang'an looked up and saw a young girl smiling at him. She was wearing neat white work clothes and her hair was neatly pulled up. She looked refreshing.He Kangan thought, come on, come and have a look in the store.There are two rectangular iron plates placed in the transparent cabinet. The bottoms are kept warm with hot water, and the dishes are still steaming.There is a small blackboard on the outside of the cupboard with the names and prices of the dishes written on it.One is mapo tofu and the other is sweet and sour eggplant, both cost 15 yuan.The spicy aroma he smelled just now was from the Mapo Tofu dish. His index finger was opened wide by the smell, so he said without hesitation: I want a Mapo Tofu rice bowl.Okay, please wait a moment, I will put the rice in it and bring it to you.Bai Xiangning quickly put the rice on the plate, and then poured a large spoonful of mapo tofu on it.Sir, your mapo tofu rice bowlHe Kangan looked at the rice bowl that was served and swallowed hard.This is the best-looking mapo tofu he has ever seen. The whole dish is red and shiny, with some emerald green onion sprinkled on top, which forms a sharp contrast with the gravy underneath. The chef's knife skills must be excellent. Not only was the tofu cut into evenly sized pieces, but it was not damaged at all and was served intact.Before he even tasted it, the spicy flavor of Mapo Tofu had already flooded into his nasal cavity, stimulating his appetite.The toppings are generous and filling, and even the rice underneath is almost invisible. Small squares of soft tofu are spread evenly on the rice, with a thin layer of Sichuan peppercorns sprinkled on top. The thick red sauce penetrates into the rice, making it tempting to look at.The neat tofu pieces are also mixed with burnt beef cubes. The beef is more umami than pork. After being oiled, it is extremely crispy.The boss is very considerate. She grinds the peppercorns into fine powder so that you won't bite into the annoying peppercorns when eating, which will affect the dining experience. When the oil is heated, the unique aroma of Sichuan peppercorn powder evaporates hundreds or thousands of times, making it more intense than the aroma of Sichuan peppercorns.The aroma of pepper and sesame rose up in the heat. He Kang'an couldn't bear it anymore and took a big spoonful of rice and stuffed it into his mouth.Hotness was the first feeling that He Kang'an experienced on his tongue.Immediately afterwards, the heat aroused numbness, like an electric shock. The numbness quickly spread to the base of the tongue, and the taste buds were instantly awakened. He pursed his lips slightly, and the soft tofu slid into his throat along with the gravy.The spicy and delicious gravy sauce blends well with the bean flavor of the tender tofu itself. After one bite, the spicy flavor takes up most of the food, but when you taste it carefully, the fragrance unique to tofu comes back.As soon as He Kang'an ate it, he knew that the boss used good rice. The rice was moderately soft and hard, and the grains were plump and elastic. Each grain of rice was wrapped in smooth tofu, charred beef cubes and rich gravy. The more delicious you eat.After taking the first bite, He Kang'an couldn't stop eating one bite after another. By the time he stopped, the rice bowl on the plate had been completely eaten, leaving only some mapo tofu sauce.Phew, so enjoyableEven though the air conditioner was turned on, He Kang'an was still sweating profusely after eating. This mapo tofu brought him unprecedented taste enjoyment, and he even felt that he could have another plate.Boss, pack me another mapo tofu and a sweet and sour eggplant rice bowl.He Kang'an thought, since Mapo tofu is so delicious, the sweet and sour eggplant must not be any different, so he packed it back for his son to try.At this time, he completely forgot what his wife had told him.Who said the food sold outside was unhygienic He just noticed that the boss had cleaned every corner of the small restaurant, and the counter where the dishes were placed was spotless and shiny. It was very hygienic at first glance. .He took two packed lunches, hummed a tune, and strolled back home.This was the first customer of Bai's small restaurant. After he left, Bai Xiangning heard a ding in her mind, and the system said:Congratulations to the host for getting a point of satisfaction. One satisfaction is equal to one point. The points can be exchanged for various props in the points mall.Bai Xiangning is interested. What props do you haveSorry host, because you don't have enough points currently, you don't have permission to view the points mall yet. But you can view it when the host accumulates ten points. Come on, host.Seeing what the system said, Bai Xiangning had no choice but to give up. Ten points meant ten points of satisfaction, which was not difficult at all for her.He Kang'an had just arrived home, and his son also opened the door and came back.Dad, what did you buy Why does it smell so goodHe Tongtong rushed to the dining table, and then opened the packing bag. As he opened it, he muttered: Mom told me not to buy me food outside. If mom finds out,He Kang'an grabbed the bag and interrupted him, "Don't eat it, I'll eat it myself."He Tongtong smiled playfully, "Oh dad, you can't eat so much, so I can help you solve it."He Kang'an snorted: I can finish it in ten minutes.After He Tongtong opened the packing box, all the aroma of rice that had been confined in the packing box suddenly came out, and his stomach growled a few times.Seeing his son's hand reaching for his portion of mapo tofu rice bowl, He Kang'an quickly replaced the one with sweet and sour eggplant next to him.You eat this sweet and sour eggplant, Mapo tofu is not suitable for children, it is too spicy.He Tongtong curled his lips and thought to himself, don't you just want to eat Mapo Tofu The last time you and I secretly ate spicy strips, you didn't say that children can't eat spicy food.He felt that his father had kept the unpalatable food for himself, so he reluctantly opened the box of sweet and sour eggplant rice bowl with a pout, and then a sweet and umami flavor that was different from Mapo Tofu floated out.Wow, looks deliciousHe suddenly no longer thought about his father's rice bowl, but couldn't wait to eat the sweet and sour eggplant rice bowl. Seeing how delicious his son was eating, He Kang'an was also greedy. He took two bites of the mapo tofu rice bowl, and then Then he looked at what his son was holding.The sweet and sour eggplant rice bowl seems to be pretty good too.Son, give daddy a taste of yours.Then I'll try dad's too.The two of them just started sharing each other's rice, and soon both rice bowls were finished.The father and son ate comfortably, leaning on the chairs and patting their bellies comfortably.At this time, the sound of opening the door sounded.Ah, mom is back

Chapter 5Quick, quick, quick, pack it up quicklyThe father and son were so frightened that they quickly threw the evidence into the trash can, not forgetting to cover it with a piece of paper to prevent it from being discovered.When Yu Xin entered the room, she found her husband and children sitting upright on the sofa. Seeing her coming back, they all turned to look at her, and then said in unison:Mom/wife; you are backYu Xin's footsteps stopped at the entrance. If something went wrong, there must be a monster. One look at the two of them's well-behaved looks and knew that they must have done something bad behind her back.She smelled it, and there seemed to be a smell of food lingering in the air, but there was no trace of cooking in the kitchen.When the father and son saw her nose twitching, they immediately froze and secretly thought something was wrong.Sure enough, the next second Yu Xin strode up to them in an aggressive manner, and then glared at He Kangan, "Are you buying unclean things for your children to eat outside again"He Kangan felt guilty, but he felt unconvinced. It's okay to say that what he bought before was junk food, but the rice bowl he bought today is healthy, hygienic, and tastes first-class. Why should he say that it is unclean foodAsk your son if the rice bowl I bought him today is delicious.He Tongtong:Why did you dump this hot potato on himBut he still answered honestly: Mom, this is the best rice bowl I have ever eaten. As he spoke, he couldn't help but smack his lips, with an afterthought expression on his face.Yu Xin was about to explode.Did you know that the rice bowl you bought for your son, the cooking oil outside is all gutter oil, and the ingredients used are not fresh What if your child has a bad stomach after eating itThe rice bowl I bought this time is really different from before. As soon as I taste it, I can tell that the ingredients are healthy and the oil is genuine. He Kang'an defended, but he and his son had already finished the rice bowl, and his wife would not believe it if he was talking nonsense. He could only say, if you don't believe it, go and try it yourself tomorrow. That shop is in the snack street. It turns out that The grocery store was closed and turned into a small restaurant.Humph, I won't go. The food I make is much more delicious than what I cook outside, Yu Xinxin said.The next second.Mom, the food you cooked is far worse than what I ate today.Yu Xin:The son said it sincerely, not realizing that he had just hit his mother's self-confidence.Children's words have no restraints, children's words have no restraints.Yu Xin stroked his chest and comforted himself.She would like to try that store tomorrow to see what it tastes like, so that both her husband and son can be so impressed.Can it taste better than hersShe didn't believe it.Bai Xiangning quickly gained ten points of satisfaction. She asked the system: What props can I buy nowThe system immediately opened the points mall. Bai Xiangning looked at it and saw that they were all very simple items. She chose one at random and wanted to see how the system would give her the props.After she selected the item she wanted, the next second something appeared in front of her, a rag.It's the kind you can buy at the grocery store for two bucks.And she just spent ten satisfaction points.The system sensed the host's dislike of it and hurriedly showed Bai Xiangning the props with higher points required.Host, look, there are a lot of good things in the mall. When you have enough points, you can buy these.The props in the system range from dozens to thousands of points. There are physical props and virtual props. The higher the points, the greater the help for opening a store. Of course, the difficulty of obtaining them also increases accordingly.If you want to get points, you have to satisfy customers. When customers are satisfied, the restaurant will open better and better, forming a virtuous cycle.Yu Xin, do you want to eat hot pot tonight I just found a new hot pot restaurant, and the reviews seem to be quite good.The colleague asked, but before Xin could answer, another colleague smiled and said: Oh, Yu Xin must go home and cook by herself, she never eats out.Yes, why did I forget about this Then let's go eatYu Xin said goodbye to them at the intersection, you go ahead, I'll buy some groceries later and go home to cook.After her colleagues walked away, Yu Xin immediately turned around and walked to the snack street.When we walked to the location of the original grocery store, we saw a newly opened restaurant.The small store was already full of people, and Yu Xin felt a little more at ease. With so many people coming to eat, the taste shouldn't be too bad.She walked into the store and found that there were only two kinds of dishes on the counter.Boss, are there only these two types Are the others sold outIt's impossible for a store to only sell two kinds of rice, rightThe young boss stood in front of the counter and smiled apologetically at her: I'm sorry, because it has just opened and I am the only one in the store, so there are relatively few dishes to choose from. More dishes will be added later.Yu Xin was a little surprised. The boss said she was the only one in the store, so who made these dishesIt's made by me, I'm both the boss and the chef. Bai Xiangning explained.Yu Xin covered her mouth, wondering why she accidentally asked what was in her heart just now.She concealed her embarrassment with a smile and looked around to see what rice bowls the other customers in the store were eating. After looking around, she found that they were eating half and half of these two types of rice bowls. The spicy and salty flavors are intertwined, and they all smell delicious.She was a little confused about which one to buy.After thinking for a long time, she realized that the boss had been waiting patiently and did not rush her. Yu Xin was even more embarrassed. She quickly said: Pack the same portion for me.She would eat one when she went back later, and then take it to work for lunch the next day.Bai Xiangning packed the two rice bowls and handed them to Yu Xin, totaling 30 yuan.After Yu Xin paid the money, Bai Xiangning smiled and said to her: Welcome to visit next timeAlthough he hasn't tasted the rice bowl yet, Yu Xin's favorable impression of this store has already increased a lot just by looking at the cleanliness of the store and the patience of the boss.When she was about to get home, Yu Xin suddenly remembered something and took out her mobile phone to make a call.Hey hubby, have you got off work yetHe Kang'an replied: No, I'm working overtime tonight and I should be back later. What's wrongHe thought his wife was going to ask him what he had for dinner, but Yu Xin seemed relieved and said, "Oh, you can take care of dinner outside. I'm losing weight and won't eat at night."Before He Kangan could ask his son what to do, Yu Xin hung up the phone.Go home quickly, the food won't taste good when it's cold.Yu Xin hurried home. Another reason why she was so anxious was to finish the meal before her husband and children came home.When she got home, she turned on the light in the living room and sat down at the dining table without even taking off her shoes. She was going to eat sweet and sour eggplant rice bowl first. Eggplant was her favorite food, but cooking it deliciously was not a good idea. An easy thing.Eggplant must be oily and flavorful to be cooked well, but if you don't control the heat well, the eggplant will taste very greasy and difficult to eat.Yu Xin often tried to make eggplant at home, but she failed every time. Either the eggplant absorbed too much oil or it was completely tasteless. Later, she gave up the idea of continuing to try after the strong protest from her husband and son.She opened the lid of the lunch box and sniffed it gently. Well, the sweet and sour taste was very authentic.The eggplant was peeled off and cut into hob pieces. Each piece was evenly coated with sauce. She picked up a piece and bit it gently. The eggplant had been fried and had a crispy surface. If she pressed harder, her teeth would sink in and the eggplant was soft. The inside was crispy on the outside and tender on the inside, and the sauce penetrated into every crevice of the eggplant. The sweet and sour sauce instantly filled her mouth, stimulating her taste buds and making her unable to help but devour it.I don't know how the boss did it. The eggplant was stuffed in the packaging box for so long, but it didn't soften at all outside.She mixed the eggplant and rice, and the dark brown sauce blended into the rice. She put it into her mouth in one bite. The soft and waxy eggplant and rice were mixed together, and it was extremely delicious.This sweet and sour eggplant dish has a strong flavor. Yu Xin chewed it slowly, and even felt like he was eating meat.She was so forgetful about eating that she didn't even notice the sound of the door opening. She was shocked when He Kang'an came up to her. She quickly tried to cover up her lunch box, which was almost full, but it was already too late.Wife, don't you eat food from outside You almost finished a box of rice bowl. He Kangan's voice was filled with a hint of pride. How about it I'm not lying to you. Doesn't this store taste particularly goodAlthough Yu Xin agreed with his opinion in her heart, she didn't want to admit it and gave a vague hum.He Kangan sat down opposite her, and then burped, hehe, I just went to eat the rice bowl, it was so delicious.Yu Xin thought of something and said to her husband: By the way, when I went to buy rice bowl today, the boss said that she was the only one in the store and the chef was herself.He Kang'an said in surprise: I didn't expect that she cooked all the dishes by herself. The boss is so good at craftsmanship at such a young age. She is really amazing. She opened the shop by herself.Yes, business is pretty good. When I went there today, the store was full.I hope the boss will provide more dishes, otherwise you will get tired of eating only two kinds sooner or later. However, there is only the boss in the store now, and I don't know if she can be busy.Don't worry about this. If the store's business is good, the boss will definitely hire more people.As soon as He Tongtong came home, he saw his parents talking about delicious food. He thought he had his own share, but when he ran to the kitchen, there was nothing there.Mom and Dad, where is my food

Chapter 6He Tongtong wailed and fell on the sofa, clutching his stomach. He was almost starving to death.Yu Xin looked at her son who was rolling around and was embarrassed to say that she had forgotten him. She struggled a lot, then took out another mapo tofu rice bowl from the refrigerator, and then looked at Chen Tongtong as if it was natural. said:What's the ghost's name Isn't this something for you to eatAs she said this, Yu Xin was crying in her heart. She originally wanted to take it to work the next day to feast on her colleagues, but her son cut off her beard.But seeing her son eating so happily, how could she feel any discomfort Food is more delicious when shared with others, not to mention giving it to her own children.She took out her phone and before eating the sweet and sour eggplant rice bowl, she couldn't help but take several photos. She chose two and then sent them to Moments with the text: The best thing I have ever eaten. The Sweet and Sour Eggplant Rice Bowl will delight eggplant loversThis circle of friends quickly received several comments, all of which were surprised.Did I read that right Xinxin ate rice bowls sold outside. Don't you never eat outsideI never expected that one day I would see Yu Xin commenting so highly on the restaurants outside. I was curious about how delicious it was, and my mouth was watering.Wow, this eggplant looks really tempting. Please tell me where this store is. I'm worried about not having a new store to eat it recently.Looking at everyone's comments, Yu Xin uniformly replied to the location of Bai's Little Restaurant, not forgetting to make another comment: Go and support the boss's business, the boss's mapo tofu rice bowl is also super delicious.Yu Xin's circle of friends brought another wave of business to Bai's small restaurant. Bai Xiangning looked at the increasing number of customers and was also considering adding new dishes. When he first opened the store, he only sold two kinds of rice bowls. Over time, customers will also want more choices, and they will get tired of eating the same food sooner or later.The previous two kinds of rice bowls were vegetarian, so Bai Xiangning planned to add a new meat dish.When she went to the vegetable market in the morning, she paid special attention to the meat section. When she reached the beef stall, she stopped.Various parts of the cow were hung in front of the stall, including long strips of beef brisket, beef tendon, and ribs. There were also beef bones, beef ribs, and beef tenderloin on the table.Come take a look at my beef. It's very fresh. It was brought from the slaughterhouse.After speaking, the boss casually took out a beef tenderloin. The meat was as fresh as he said, and the muscle tissue of the meat was even beating.Boss, how much does this beef tenderloin costThe boss said boldly: "45 per pound, you can buy as much as you want, I'll make it cheaper for you"Bai Xiangning has already thought about what to cook with this beef tenderloin, but since it is new, she doesn't plan to buy too many raw materials. After thinking for a moment, she made a mark on the freshest beef tenderloin.Bring me these.okayWith the tip of the boss's knife, a neat beef tenderloin was cut off. When weighed, it was exactly four pounds.Bai Xiangning went to buy three eggs again and went back with her hands full.Her physical strength is much better now than when she first came here. At first she couldn't even lift a pot, but now she can maintain four pounds of beef in her left hand and three plates of eggs in her right hand without changing her expression or heartbeat.Back in the store, she arranged the eggs neatly and then started processing the beef.After rinsing the surface of the beef tenderloin, she took out a kitchen knife and started to slice the meat. The Baixiang Ning knife was very good at slicing the meat. Not only did it slice the meat very quickly, but each slice of meat was sliced uniformly and evenly.If you want the beef to taste good and chewy, you must cut the fiber of the beef against the grain, so that the beef will be tender.In a short time, all the ingredients were processed. She looked at the time and saw that it was almost three o'clock.There are not many ingredients now, and she can process them faster by herself. However, considering the later development of the small restaurant, she feels that she needs to recruit an assistant now. Otherwise, she will be the only one in the store, cooking and serving as a waiter. too busy.She opened the system to see if there were any props in the system that could help her, and she found one.A reliable helperPoints required: 500Bai Xiangning decided to save points to redeem this prop. If there was one more person in the store to help, she would have more time to research new dishes, which would greatly relieve her pressure.Moreover, it is not easy to recruit people now, and it is even more difficult to recruit a long-term and capable person. But now, with only 500 points, the system can find a reliable helper for her, which is a great deal.She calculated that according to the current progress, she would be able to save five hundred points in less than a month.Bai Xiangning took off her apron and planned to take a rest before starting the formal production.She leaned on the recliner for a while, and her phone rang. She picked it up and saw that it was Chen Feng calling.Xiang Ning, I heard from my parents that your store has opened. It just so happens that I have a day off today to support you.Chen Feng's voice came through the microphone.OK, you're always welcome. Bai Xiangning said with a smile.Hahaha, I'll be over right away, I've been thinking about itLess than an hour after putting down the phone, Chen Feng came over. When he arrived, Bai Xiangning opened the door. Seeing him coming, Bai Xiangning greeted him with a smile: You are here, come in and sit down.Before Chen Feng went in, he smelled the aroma of the food inside. He sniffed, it smelled so good.He couldn't help but think of the delicious fried noodles and the rice on the table last time. He still couldn't forget the taste, so he was full of expectations for the food in Bai Xiangning's restaurant before he came.As long as it comes from the hands of his sister Xiang Ning, the taste will definitely be the same.You came just in time, I just served a new dish today.Chen Feng looked at the transparent window. There were three rectangular plates neatly arranged inside. On the small blackboard next to it was written: Today's new beef rice bowl with eggs is 20 yuan.He is the only one in the store at this time, which means that if he orders this new dish, he will be the first one to taste it.Although I couldn't be the first customer of Bai's restaurant, I was lucky to be the first to taste the new dishes.Although the other two kinds of rice bowls looked very tempting, in line with the principle of eating the new and not the old, Chen Feng chose the beef rice bowl with smooth egg without hesitation.It's not too late to eat the other two kinds later.After the rice bowl was served, the aroma of hot rice went straight into Chen Feng's nose.Fresh beef does not need to be added with cooking wine. You only need to marinate the ginger slices for a while, then add light soy starch and mix well. Finally, seal it with cooking oil and stir-fry it until it is half cooked, then scoop it out and mix it with the egg liquid.The so-called smooth egg is to use the residual heat of the pot to slowly solidify the egg liquid into a smooth and tender state. This method will not make the eggs become too old, but retains the moist texture of the egg liquid.The smooth eggs have a golden color and rich egg flavor. Just by looking at them, you can imagine how tender the eggs are.Fragrant, so fragrantThe impact at close range made him unable to wait for a moment, so he blew a few blows casually and stuffed a large spoonful of rice into his mouth.Mmm, delicious, so deliciousThe high temperature causes the surface of the beef to quickly char, while the abundant juice is still firmly locked inside. After entering the mouth, the juice immediately splashes out. After touching the smooth egg, it evokes a unique aroma, the aroma of beef and egg. We are closely connected, regardless of you or me.The beef is cut against the grain, the fascia is completely cut off, and the wrapping of eggs makes the beef more tender and smooth. Even the elderly or children with bad teeth can eat it effortlessly.Chen Feng took a sip, and the salty and fresh taste overflowed to every corner of his mouth. At this time, paired with a mouthful of rice, it was really delicious.

Chapter 7Chen Feng finished the full portion of rice bowl in just three strokes.He touched his stomach and found that he was only seventy percent full, so he turned his attention to the other two rice bowls. Should he eat Mapo Tofu Rice Bowl or Sweet and Sour Eggplant Rice BowlWhen Chen Feng was debating whether to order another rice bowl, he received a WeChat message: [Brother Feng, we have chosen a few restaurants where to have dinner this year and are waiting for your decision.]Then I scrolled, and several more messages popped up, all of which were hotel positioning.The person who sent him the message was his brother who was doing decoration work together. He had been working with him for five or six years. We all have a team building dinner every year.After receiving the news, Chen Feng remembered that it was indeed time for team building this year.Zhao Panyang discovered that several of his restaurants are Internet celebrity restaurants. He has also visited some of them, but they are all the type that he doesn't like and doesn't like the food. He probably invests all his money in advertising.He looked around and didn't decide which restaurant to go to. Either he disliked the location or the food. Anyway, there was no one he liked.Although Chen Feng himself is not too picky about food, after all, it is a gathering of brothers and everyone will be happy to choose a restaurant with delicious food.Chen Feng's thinking changed from what rice bowl to eat to which restaurant to choose for dinner.He glanced at the display window with dishes, and thought regretfully, it's a pity that Xiang Ning's house only sells rice bowls at the moment, otherwise wouldn't this be the best place for a dinner partyXiang Ning's craftsmanship is so good, which store outside can compare with itAlthough the noodles with fried bean paste I had last time and the beef rice with smooth egg this time were both very common, Bai Xiangning's skillful hands can make ordinary ingredients delicious.I really want to eat more of her dishes.It would be great if she would be willing to host their dinner party this time.This idea was strong and urgent, and quickly occupied his brain.He hesitated no longer and stood up suddenly.It's not the peak dining period yet, so there aren't many people in the store.Bai Xiangning had just served a customer a meal and was free at the moment.Chen Feng walked to Bai Xiangning and told Bai Xiangning what he had just thought.There was a hope in his tone that even he was unaware of.It's okay, it's okay, even if it's for the sake of his parents, he must agree.Perhaps his too strong voice was heard by Bai Xiangning, and she agreed after a little thought.Chen Feng and the others planned to have dinner together at noon, and her restaurant only opened in the evening, so there was enough time.Besides, there were not many of them. There were only nine people in the decoration team including Chen Feng, just enough for one table. Cooking a table of meals was no big deal for Bai Xiangning, so she agreed to Chen Feng without much hesitation.When will you come overChen Feng discussed it with his brothers and set the time for the dinner in a week.Ok, no problem. Do you have any requirements for the dishes Do you have any dietary restrictions or special cravingsThis was Bai Xiangning's first private dinner since she came to this world, and she took it more seriously, but Chen Feng didn't seem to care at all about what she cooked, and said boldly:Xiang Ning, you can do whatever you want, we will eat whatever you do.Chen Feng's words were not polite. He felt from the bottom of his heart that whatever Bai Xiangning cooked was delicious. When he thought about having dinner together in a week, he wanted to faint immediately and wake up again a week later.If he didn't have to take care of everyone in the decoration team's time, he would definitely have an appointment with Bai Xiangning tomorrow, no, todayBut fortunately, he can still eat the rice bowl.So should I order mapo tofu or sweet and sour eggplantWhen he finally remembered this problem, the three large dishes on the counter were gone, leaving only some soup.

What did he miss Why did all the kung fu dishes disappear after a whileNoticing his surprised look, Bai Xiangning explained: There have been customers coming in just now, so I'm just serving food and talking to you.Chen Feng had just been thinking about the dinner party and didn't notice the arrival of other customers. Now that all the dishes are sold out, he can only swallow his greedy food.It doesn't matter, he will come back tomorrowEver since Yu Xin personally tasted the rice bowl at Bai's Little Restaurant, she has never stopped her husband and son from eating it. On the contrary, sometimes when she works overtime, she will ask He Kang'an to pack it for her and take it home.Yu Xin, who never eats in restaurants outside, not only broke the habit, but also became addicted to it, and even made her office colleagues fall in love with the rice bowls at Bai's Little Restaurant.Hey, you also had rice bowls from a small restaurant today.Yu Xin and her colleagues in the office all tacitly understood that as long as they talked about a small restaurant, they must be referring to Bai's small restaurant.Yeah, you tooYu Xin and her colleagues tacitly took out their lunch boxes. As expected, they were all filled with rice bowls, but the colleague's was Mapo Tofu Rice Bowl, while Yu Xin's was the new Slippery Egg Beef Rice Bowl.Ah, this is the new beef rice bowl with smooth egg in the restaurant. It looks delicious.Yu Xin said: Yes, why didn't you buy the beef rice bowl with smooth egg I remember that you really like beef.My colleague burst into tears. Do you think I don't want to When I left work yesterday, I only had Mapo Tofu left. If I had been a few minutes later, I wouldn't even have had to eat Mapo Tofu.When Yu Xin heard this, she suddenly felt that she was quite smart. If she hadn't asked her husband to help buy it yesterday, she wouldn't be able to eat the beef rice bowl with smooth egg.Let me share it with you. Yu Xinzhu said that the relationship between colleagues in the office is very harmonious, and they often share lunch together.Colleague, I'm sorry. That's not good. Share it with me. What if you don't have enough to eatOops, the portion of rice bowl is so big, I'm sure it's enough for you, so don't be polite to me. I see your mouth is drooling, and you said you don't want to eat it.So my colleagues stopped being polite.Yu Xin gave her colleague several large spoonfuls of rice bowl, and finally added a separate spoonful of beef with smooth egg to her.My colleague took a bite and his eyes immediately filled with tears. "Uuuuuuuuuuuuuuuuuuuuuuuuuuuuuuuuuuuuuuuuuuuu uuu"Damn, what's the point of this Why don't we all share the delicious foodYu Xin took a bite of the beef rice bowl with smooth egg as she spoke. As soon as she took her mouth, her expression froze.This is too delicious, rightShe even regretted sharing so much rice bowl with her colleagues just now.While she was crying silently in her heart, she took big gulps into her mouth without delaying her meal at all.It's okay, she won't work overtime tonight, she will buy another one herself and eat enoughThe colleague obviously wanted to go with her. As soon as they finished eating, they said to Xin: I feel like I didn't eat enough. Let's go to the store and order another one tonight.As a beef lover, she thinks the beef in the egg-slippery beef is the best she has ever tasted.Although the beef has been cut into thin slices, the unique meat flavor of the beef has not diminished at all. The taste becomes more intense under the high temperature cooking, and melts in the mouth together with the tender eggs, forming a wonderful taste experience.The overnight meal packed the night before is so delicious even if it is reheated. If you eat it on site, it will definitely taste twice as good.Yu Xin readily agreed: Okay.The two of them were ready to go before they got off work, organized everything, and rushed out when the clock hands reached six o'clock.

Chapter 8The business of the small restaurant is really good. They came right after get off work today without any delay. However, when they arrived, the restaurant was almost full.Yu Xin quickly grabbed the last table and sat down with his colleagues.Boss Bai, please order two portions of beef rice bowl with smooth egg.Yu Xin had been thinking about it all afternoon, waiting to get off work to have a good time. She had just said not long ago that she wanted to lose weight by not eating at night, but now she had already forgotten the idea of losing weight.How can you have the energy to lose weight if you don't eat enoughThe food in the small restaurant is so delicious, how could she miss it just because she lost weight The loss would be too great.The taste of eating it freshly in the store is indeed better than taking it home. The rice bowl is steaming with fresh heat, the beef and eggs are more tender and smooth, and the smooth egg is worthy of being called a smooth egg. It slides into the throat almost as soon as you eat it.Yu Xin usually chats about some gossip when eating with her colleagues during lunch break, but at this time, neither of them focused on anything other than eating.I'm afraid that if I say another word, my meal will go cold.They really wanted to restrain themselves from eating and taste the ultimate deliciousness slowly, but the smooth egg beef was so delicious that they were tempted to take one bite after another and couldn't stop.When I finally put down the spoon, the bottom of the plate was already clean.The beef with smooth egg is not a dish with a lot of soup. The small amount of gravy has just been mixed into the rice, so now there is no soup left at the bottom of the plate.After eating, the two of them breathed a sigh of relief.Their stomachs feel very satisfied. Being filled with delicious food is a completely different experience than being filled with unpleasant food.Why didn't Yu Xin like eating out beforeBecause when she ate out, she either used dirty oil, which caused her to have diarrhea after eating, or the food was not cooked to a high standard and was not as delicious as what she cooked herself. Eating such a meal is a torture to the stomach.But small restaurants are different.Although it is just a small shop with an ordinary name and an ordinary storefront, the owner has the ability to transform decay into magic and can make such a small shop in a not-so-good location so special.Seeing the boss constantly shuttling between customers, cleaning tables, and serving meals to customers, Yu Xin couldn't help but said to her colleagues: Boss Bai is working too hard. There are so many customers in the store, and she has to do all this by herself. To do thatThe guests at the next table just finished eating and left. Bai Xiangning came over to wipe the table, and then heard what Yu Xin said. Yu Xin was also a regular customer, so Bai Xiangning explained one more sentence:I have plans to recruit people. Once I recruit people, I will have more time to prepare new dishes.Yu Xin said in surprise: Boss Bai is planning to serve a new dish, will it still be made into a rice bowlThe rice bowl is actually quite delicious, fast and convenient, but it is too fast-food style, so if you want to have a meal with family and friends, a small restaurant is not suitable.If there are many people, I still hope to order dishes. After all, no one at a dinner party would choose to eat rice bowls together.Yu Xin was thinking about it in her heart, but fortunately Bai Xiangning answered her question immediately.Of course I won't make rice bowls anymore. I make rice bowls now because I'm the only one in the store and there's not enough manpower. I plan to make some separate dishes in the future, so you can order them when you come to the store.Bai Xiangning's answer immediately aroused Yu Xin's expectations. She then asked: Boss, when will you recruit people I see there is no recruitment notice posted at the door of the store. You posted the recruitment online. AnnouncementYu Xin's words really stunned Bai Xiangning.She just checked the points she had earned so far, and it was only a few dozen points away from reaching 500. It was probably just in the past two days. When you get 500 points, in what form will that reliable helper appearWhat does she need to do Does it mean that, like Yu Xin said, she has to put up a recruitment notice before anyone will comeSeeing Bai Xiangning frowning, Yu Xin thought that she had asked too many questions, so she quickly waved her hand and apologized, "I'm sorry, boss, I just asked casually."Bai Xiangning immediately relaxed her brows and said with a smile: It's okay, I was just thinking about something.She decided not to post the recruitment notice yet. Anyway, she would soon have enough 500 points, and she would wait until she finished redeeming the props.-Tongtong, my deskmate Wang Jiexi suddenly called He Tongtong's name out of nowhere.He Tongtong is lowering his head and concentrating on his homework. He has become more serious about his studies recently because his mother said that as long as he does his homework well every day, he will buy him rice bowls from the Bai Family Restaurant.He Tongtong also worked hard for a bite to eat. He previewed carefully before class, listened carefully in class, and reviewed carefully after class. His academic performance skyrocketed, and some classmates even asked him questions during class.At this time, he heard his deskmate calling him. He didn't even raise his head. His eyes were still focused on the math paper in front of him. What's wrong Why are you calling meWang Jiexi stretched out his hand and quickly flicked He Tongtong's chin while he wasn't paying attention.He Tongtong's fleshy chin trembled.Wang Jiexi's last hit, Tongtong, what delicious food has your mother made for you recently Look at your double chin.He Tongtong finally stopped writing in his hand and turned to look at his deskmate, hum, my mother didn't prepare me any delicious food.Then youWang Jiexi looked He Tongtong up and down, scanning his double chin, then his belly that could still be seen even though it was obscured by the loose school uniform, and finally stopped at his fatter face.He Tongtong naturally understood what his deskmate's look meant, so why didn't he just try another way to call him fatOh, what do you know Boys are cute only if they are fat.He was not angry at all, but said with a little pride: Huh, my parents recently discovered a super delicious shop outside and often buy me meals there.Wang Jiexi didn't seem to believe it, so he confirmed again. You just said that your parents and your mother often buy you food from that store.No, my mother has bought it for me more times than my father.Wang Jiexi's pupils suddenly trembled, and he looked at He Tongtong with an expression like "What's going on Your mother actually bought you a meal from outside. Has she completely given up on you as her son"He and He Tongtong have been classmates since kindergarten. He knows that He Tongtong's mother never allows him to eat outside because she thinks the food outside is very unhygienic. Once before, he took He Tongtong secretly to eat fried skewers and was caught, causing He Tongtong to get scolded a lot.As a result, He Tongtong actually said that his mother not only agreed with him eating out, but would even buy it for him herself.Wang Jiexi's shock only lasted for a few seconds, and then he asked excitedly: So, from now on, we can eat fried skewers openly.To enjoy fried skewers, two people have to eat them together. He always goes there alone, which is so boring.Unexpectedly, He Tongtong was not as excited as him at all. He drooped his head on the table and said wiltedly: "That still doesn't work. My mother only allows me to eat food from that store, but she still won't let me eat anything else."He then raised his head again and added, "But my mother is just worrying. I don't want to eat food from other families at all. To be honest, I don't even want to eat the food she cooks now."ahWhat store has such magicAs soon as he said this, He Tongtong became excited. You don't know how delicious the rice bowl in that store is. I have never eaten such delicious rice bowl.Bah bah bah, He Tongtong said a lot of compliments like he was pouring beans.Wang Jiexi was amazed when he heard this.He had never known that He Tongtong was so eloquent. It seemed that he had spent his whole life praising a small restaurant.Although he felt that He Tongtong's words were exaggerated. No matter how delicious a rice bowl restaurant could be, Wang Jiexi was still greedy. It was almost lunch time, and Wang Jiexi felt that his stomach was full. In protest.He wanted to try that shop.But the next second, He Tongtong said: How are you, do you really want to eatHe Tongtong puffed up his chest proudly, as if he felt that his tablemate would definitely eat it because of his strong recommendation.Seeing his appearance, Wang Jiexi suddenly became arrogant.Humph, I don't want to eat it. Who hasn't eaten rice bowl before What's so strange about it, he said vehemently.He Tongtong was unconvinced. How do you know if you haven't eaten it Maybe you will think about it every day after eating it. He was so angry that his cheeks bulged. The restaurant was so delicious, and he would never allow anyone to belittle it.Not to be outdone, Wang Jiexi uttered the harshest words for his age.If I eat it, I will be a puppyHe Tongtong:you win.It's better to concentrate on doing the questions. If he does well in school, his mother will continue to buy him rice bowls from the small restaurant.He didn't want to continue talking to his childish roommate.Seeing that He Tongtong stopped paying attention to him, Wang Jiexi first clasped his fingers for a while, and then started playing with his pen. During this period, He Tongtong did the questions without raising his head.The thought of going to that restaurant has been lingering in Wang Jiexi's mind, like a kitten's claws scratching in his heart.But he had already said harsh words in front of He Tongtong, how could he break his wordsWang Jiexi suppressed the thoughts that he shouldn't have had, but it was no use. After suppressing them for a while, Wang Jiexi finally couldn't help but ask:Tongtong, you just said that it was your parents who bought the rice bowl for you, right If it was He Tongtong's parents who went to buy it, then he doesn't have to worry. Even if he goes to eat, he won't run into He Tongtong.yes. He Tongtong responded.When Wang Jiexi heard this, the villain in his heart jumped so high.greatHe decided to try that shop tonight after schoolThe school bell rings.In the past, Wang Jiexi would go out to school with He Tongtong, but today, in order not to reveal his fault, Wang Jiexi made an excuse and ran away as soon as school was over.ten minutes later.Wang JiexiWhen he heard a familiar voice, Wang Jiexi, who was immersed in eating, suddenly looked up.He Tongtong was standing at the door looking at him with wide eyes.Didn't you say you had diarrhea today Why are you here

Chapter 9At the same time that He Tongtong asked this question, Wang Jiexi dropped the spoon filled with rice on the plate, and a few grains of rice spilled onto the table.What I fear most is that the air suddenly becomes quiet.Wang Jiexi's face turned red. He regretted it now, very much.Why did he put down his harsh words and say that he would be a puppy if he came to eat at this restaurantNow that He Tongtong has caught him, he will be completely embarrassed.While Wang Jiexi was struggling in his heart, he picked up the spoon and scooped out another big spoonful of rice and stuffed it into his mouth. Mmm, it was delicious.He Tongtong also ordered a rice bowl and sat down in front of Wang Jiexi. Wang Jiexi looked at him carefully while eating, but He Tongtong seemed to have forgotten about it and couldn't wait to start eating after sitting down. .When they both had almost eaten, Wang Jiexi remembered something. He asked He Tongtong: Didn't you say that your parents buy you rice bowls every time Why did you come here by yourself todayHe Tongtong glanced at him and said: Didn't you also say that you had diarrhea and wanted to go home earlyHey Hey. Wang Jiexi laughed dryly to cover up his embarrassment.My parents worked overtime today, so they asked me to come over and buy food. Seeing that Wang Jiexi's plate was clean, He Tongtong said proudly: Isn't the rice bowl in the small restaurant deliciousWang Jiexi nodded honestly. If he didn't believe it before eating it, he was completely impressed by the rice bowl after eating it.He now fully understood why He Tongtong said that he didn't even like the food cooked by his mother after eating in a small restaurant. Wang Jiexi thought about it carefully and realized that his mother's cooking was really not as good as that of this small restaurant.The two have a tacit understanding of being classmates for many years. After looking at each other, they said in unison: Then let's come over to eat every night from now on.Ding ding, congratulations to the host for successfully obtaining 500 points.At around nine o'clock in the morning, Bai Xiangning was cleaning the store when a system notification suddenly sounded in her mind.Now, please host go to the points mall to choose your favorite props.Finally accumulated enough points.Bai Xiangning opened the points mall and decisively chose the option she had long thought about: a reliable helper.After pressing the OK key, nothing happens.She stood there and waited for a while, but the surroundings were still quiet and no one appeared.Well, why is it different from what she thoughtThe system said quietly: Could it be that the host thought that he would come out transformed into a living personIs not itBai Xiangning remembered the question Yu Xin asked her before. Did she have to post a recruitment notice at the door firstShe went to the second floor, found a piece of white paper from above, then took a black pen and wrote a few big words on it: recruitment notice. After writing, I made the edges of the words thicker to make them look more eye-catching.She shook the paper twice and then walked down the stairs.Just as he was about to walk to the door, a person walked in from outside.Bai Xiangning thought it was a customer and subconsciously said: Sorry, our store hasn't opened yet.Then a somewhat nervous voice sounded.Well, I want to ask, are you recruiting people hereThis was a woman who was about forty years old and dressed very simply. After saying that, she looked at Bai Xiangning with some restraint.Before Bai Xiangning could speak, the sound of the system appeared in her mind again, clang clang clang, a reliable helper had appeared.Bai Xiangning understood clearly that it had appeared in this way. She picked up the recruitment notice she had just written. It seemed that this piece of paper was no longer needed.The woman opposite was holding on to her clothes in embarrassment, but suddenly she saw the recruitment notice in Bai Xiangning's hand, and a glimmer of hope immediately appeared in her eyes.She said cautiously: Since we are recruiting people, do you think I can do it I work very quickly and will never be lazy.After saying this, she shut her mouth again, as if she didn't know how to promote herself.But Bai Xiangning didn't need her to say anything more. Even without a system, she could see that the woman in front of her was very honest and someone who could help.May I have your nameThe woman replied softly: My name is Qiao Ping, I am thirty-six years old.Bai Xiangning learned from Qiao Ping that she had just moved here from the next city and was alone with a ten-year-old daughter.She said no more, and Bai Xiangning didn't continue to ask.With just a few words, Bai Xiangning also knew that Qiao Ping's life must not be easy, otherwise she wouldn't look several years older than her actual age. Her clothes were very simple, and the edges of her sleeves were even washed white.After briefly talking about her own situation, Qiao Ping looked at Bai Xiangning a little uneasily, as if she was afraid that she would think her conditions were not good and would not want to recruit her. But she was not good at lying, so she just subconsciously told the truth.But Bai Xiangning didn't have any scruples. Instead, she smiled kindly at her and said, "My surname is Bai. I am the owner of this store. We will work together from now on."It took Qiao Ping a while to realize what Bai Xiangning meant.She said in surprise: Then I can work hereBai Xiangning nodded with a smile, and then explained the basic salary and benefits. The probation period is one month, and the salary is 5,000. After becoming a full-time employee, the salary will be 6,000, and five insurances and one housing fund will be paid. There are four days off every month. If you work overtime, the overtime pay is 200 per day.Considering that catering work is intensive and there is relatively little rest time, Bai Xiangning's salary is higher than the average salary.Do you think the treatment is acceptableQiao Ping did not hesitate: It's absolutely okayTo be honest, she had almost given up hope before coming here. She asked every shop along the street, but was rejected by them all. Some bosses even yelled at her, saying she was affecting their business and told her to get out immediately.But she had just arrived in this city, was unfamiliar with the place, and was not very good at surfing the Internet. In order to make a living, I can only accompany my smiling face and go door to door to ask questions.This store is at the corner of the street. Qiao Ping asked all the stores in front of her before arriving here. After countless rejections, she finally got a job opportunity here.Moreover, the salary Boss Bai offered her was so high, which was completely beyond her expectation.Qiao Ping cherished this hard-won opportunity. Just as Bai Xiangning said she wanted to hire her, she picked up the mop behind the door and said, "Boss Bai, I'll mop the floor."Before Bai Xiangning could say anything, Qiao Ping had already started mopping the ground.Although she didn't talk much, she worked quickly. Within two minutes, the ground was clean and bright.Qiao Ping took the used mop and asked: Boss Bai, is there a bathroom here I'm going to wash the mop.Bai Xiangning pointed out the location of the bathroom to her, and Qiao Ping walked to the bathroom again and started running water to wash the mop.Five minutes later, Qiao Ping walked out, wiped the sweat from her forehead briefly, and then said: Boss Bai, if there is anything else I can help with, just ask me, I can do any job.Bai Xiangning laughed. She took the washed mop from Qiao Ping's hand, and then said: There is nothing to do for the time being. Just sit down and rest.Qiao Ping looked at her empty hands and said eagerly: How can that be done If you hire me, of course I will have to do more work, otherwise what will happenBai Xiangning pushed her onto the chair, "Okay, okay, I know you are in a hurry to work, but it's almost lunch time now, let's wait until after dinner."Qiao Ping stood up again, Boss Bai, are you going to cook I'll help you.Bai Xiangning didn't know whether to laugh or cry, but she didn't refuse. Okay, then you come with me.Since there were only two of them eating at noon, Bai Xiangning planned to simply stir-fry two vegetables and make a soup.With Qiao Ping's help, Bai Xiangning quickly prepared lunch in only twenty minutes.Eat quickly. Seeing that Qiao Ping was stunned and had no intention of moving her chopsticks, Bai Xiangning said.Oh, okay, okay. Qiao Ping picked up the chopsticks, but didn't pick up the food.Bai Xiangning smiled and said, "Don't be cautious, we can eat as much as we want with this package of rice."Qiao Ping looked flattered. She never expected that Boss Bai not only offered her a high salary, but also included meals. She would get a job with such a good salary. What kind of luck did she haveBai Xiangning fried shredded green pepper pork and coriander beef, and also made tomato and egg soup, all simple home-cooked dishes.But Qiao Ping's eyes became a little red as she ate.She didn't have much money in her pocket when she came to this city with her daughter, and even less after renting a house. She often went hungry and satiated herself, just to give her daughter better food.It had been a long time since she had had a decent meal.But now there was a warm meal that Boss Bai had just prepared in front of her.Boss Bai let her eat as much as she wanted.What's wrong with youSeeing that Qiao Ping remained silent, Bai Xiangning asked with concern.Qiao Ping has just arrived. As a boss, it is very important for her to always pay attention to the emotions of her employees. After all, only when employees are in a good mood will they be motivated to work.It's nothing, I, I just feel like I'm dreaming. Qiao Ping blinked hard and pushed back her tears.She has found a job now and her life will get better and better. She should be happy.Qiao Ping stuffed a big mouthful of rice into her mouth as if to cover up.Even such a simple meal felt like a rare delicacy to her. Boss Bai's hands are like magic, and he can easily give the food the most delicious taste.Qiao Ping thought of her daughter. It would be great if her daughter could also eat such delicious food.She hesitated for a moment and asked in a low voice: Boss Bai, can I pack up the remaining dishes and take them back The food you cooked is so delicious. I want to give it to my daughter to try.After talking about it, her voice became smaller and smaller, and her head became lower and lower.She felt a little regretful when she asked. Did Boss Bai think that she was too pushy It was not enough to pack her a meal. She also thought about taking it back to her daughter.Bai Xiangning's gentle voice sounded, do you live far from hereNot far away, in the community behind. The rent there is very cheap, a price she can afford.Then it won't be packed.Qiao Ping lowered her head again. Sure enough, her request was too much, which made Boss Bai unhappy.But then, Bai Xiangning said: When you get off work, put some fresh and hot meals in the store and take them back.There wasn't much food left at lunch, so I couldn't eat it even if I packed it back.Is it really possible Qiao Ping looked at Bai Xiangning excitedly and confirmed again.sure.Qiao Ping thanked Bai Xiangning gratefully.Not only was Boss Bai not angry because of her request, he was also very considerate and gave her a better choice. Any other boss would have kicked her out.Qiao Ping made up her mind that she would work hard in the store with all her strength from now on, and she would never let down Boss Bai's kindness.Bai Xiangning didn't think Qiao Ping's request was too much. As a mother, it's normal to miss her children. Anyway, the food is provided in the store, so if Qiao Ping eats more, it doesn't mean much to her. Influence.

Chapter 10There are two days left before Chen Feng and Bai Xiangning's scheduled dinner date.There are nine people coming in total, so Bai Xiangning plans to cook nine dishes. In her free time these days, she was thinking about the specific dishes to cook. During this period, she also asked Qiao Ping for her opinion, but no matter what she said, Qiao Ping said it was okay and had no reference at all.Ever since Bai Xiangning agreed to let Qiao Ping pack food for her daughter that day, Qiao Ping has become a loyal supporter of Bai Xiangning. No matter what she says, Qiao Ping agrees.

No matter what Bai Xiangning wants to do, Qiao Ping They all got done first, of course, except for cooking.After several days of consideration, Bai Xiangning finally decided on the dishes for the dinner.On the day of the dinner, in order to buy the freshest and best ingredients one step ahead of others, Bai Xiangning and Qiao Ping got up an hour earlier than usual.Since there were a lot of things to buy, the two of them dragged a cart containing vegetables to the vegetable market. Then they would just load the vegetables and meat into the cart, so they didn't have to carry them, which would save effort.They had to get up early to go to the vegetable market. When they arrived, there were only a few people in the huge vegetable market, and the large group of people buying vegetables had not yet arrived, so they had plenty of time to choose ingredients.Bai Xiangning selects carefully. After all, the quality of the ingredients directly determines the quality of the finished dish. If the ingredients are not good, no matter how good her cooking skills are, the food she makes will not taste that good.Therefore, buying good ingredients is the first step to a successful dish.The two of them wandered around the vegetable market for almost an hour before buying all the ingredients they needed. Bai Xiangning looked at the time and saw that it was only early seven o'clock.Come on, let's go back to the store.Bai Xiangning is extremely satisfied with Qiao Ping as her assistant. She does things without procrastination and is quick with her hands and feet. When Bai Xiangning asks her to cut vegetables and meat, she can handle it quickly.When it was almost eleven o'clock, Bai Xiangning received a call from Chen Feng, Xiangning, we still have about half an hour to arrive.Chen Feng's side was very noisy. He must have been driving on the road, and he could still vaguely hear the whistle.After hanging up the phone, Zhao Panyang, who was sitting in the passenger seat, said: Brother Feng, I have never heard of the store we are going to this time. Is it reliableSeveral people sitting in the back seat all showed the same skeptical expression.Definitely reliableThe last time he went to renovate Bai Xiangning's store, several people did not go together because they were busy with other decoration projects, and then missed the extremely delicious lunch.There was no room for one car, so they came in two cars. Unfortunately, the people in the same car as Chen Feng were all people who had never eaten Bai Xiangning's food last time.But I can't even find this store online. It can't be a shady store.When they usually go out to eat, they will habitually search online for reviews first, and only then eat if the reviews are good. If there are more negative reviews, they will not consider it.But the store that Brother Feng wanted to take them to today didn't even have any reviews online.What's scarier than having bad reviewsOf course there is no evaluation.Everyone was beating their hearts out, wondering if Brother Feng chose this little-known shop just because it was cheap.But the decoration team has taken on a lot of work recently, so they can't even afford a meal.Chen Feng patted his chest and said: You still can't believe that Brother Feng's store is unique in the world.Half an hour later.Xiang Ning, here we comeBai Xiangning walked to the door after hearing the sound, and everyone's eyes suddenly lit up.Is this the bossHow come there is such a young and good-looking bossIn order not to interfere with cooking, Bai Xiangning tied her hair up high, completely revealing her fair and beautiful face.Several people who had not seen Bai Xiangning last time turned to look at Chen Feng and asked why Brother Feng had to come here to eat. It was because they saw the landlady looking good-looking.Chen Feng didn't notice the other people's eyes at all. He was only thinking about eating.Bai Xiangning smiled and said to them: Come in quickly.Oh my god, the boss lady looks better when she smilesThe single young men in the decoration team couldn't help but blush, and then they pretended to be casual and started arranging their clothes and hairstyle.There were no other customers at noon, so Bai Xiangning put together several tables on the first floor in advance to form a large table, enough for nine people to sit.Chen Feng had no objection to this, but the other members of the decoration team started to murmur in their hearts when they saw this. Doesn't this store even have a private roomThis is too shabby, rightThey immediately had no expectations for this dinner.Although the boss lady is very good-looking, her appearance that is too young and good-looking will make people doubt her craftsmanship.The method is 80% not delicious.Except for Chen Feng and the few people who came last time, everyone else had the same idea in their minds.However, since the store was highly recommended by Chen Feng and they had already come here, they naturally couldn't show off their faces and had to sit down reluctantly.Bai Xiangning naturally noticed their expressions, and she didn't say much. After all, the current conditions of the small restaurant were indeed limited, and it was normal for others to have their own thoughts.When all the dishes were served, everyone exclaimed that they looked delicious.Zhao Panyang was the first to move his chopsticks. He moved so eagerly that it was impossible to tell that he had disliked the small restaurant before.Because what was placed in front of him happened to be his favorite dish, sweet and sour pork ribs.The pork ribs are deep red and shiny, and each piece is evenly coated with rich sauce.But what are these round things insideThis is plum pork ribs. I made some improvements on the basis of sweet and sour pork ribs and made this plum pork ribs.As the chef, Bai Xiangning explained at the right time.It turned out to be Hua Mei.No wonder there is a very special smell in the air that is different from the sour smell of vinegar. It seems that it is the fragrance of plum blossoms.Zhao Panyang picked up a piece of ribs.After taking just one bite, he narrowed his eyes in intoxication.The first thing that comes into contact with the tongue is the sauce on the ribs, which is sour and sweet, with a hint of the unique fragrance of plums.Almost instantly, his appetite was whetted and he wanted to eat everything on the plate.The addition of plum blossoms adds a unique flavor to the whole dish. It tastes slightly sweet and sour, but not greasy at all. Moreover, plums can make the meat of the ribs more tender and can better absorb the flavor of the sauce.The prejudice just now disappeared after eating this bite of Huamei Spare Ribs.Who said this store can't be goodOh, it's his tasteless colleagues.In this case, then this plate of plum pork ribs belongs to him, hahahaWhyWhy is there only the last piece of the plate full of spareribs that was just leftZhao Panyang was dumbfounded. When he looked up, he realized that everyone on the table had bulging mouths. There was one who was even more outrageous. He clearly had a sparerib in his mouth and actually had one on his chopsticks.How unreasonableZhao Panyang had quick eyes and quick hands, and quickly put the last rib into his bowl while others were not paying attention.Fang Wenjun, who was sitting next to him, immediately shouted, "Ah, that's the last piece. I was just about to pick it up."Hum hum, eating is all about hand speed, who told you to move slowlyHis smug look makes you want to beat him to death.Fang Wenjun was not willing to be outdone.He aimed at another dish on the table, dry-pot fat intestines.He used to love eating sausages, and the best restaurant in his memory was a local restaurant next to where he went to college. The sausages were delicious. Unfortunately, not long after eating, the owner of that store went out of business due to health reasons.Later, he ate sausages made by other places, but they were far inferior to the one next to the school. In all these years, he has never eaten sausages as delicious as that store.As time went by, he rarely ordered this dish outside. Anyway, he was disappointed when he tasted it. The delicious food in the past may only stay in his memory.He didn't expect that there would be dry pot sausages at today's dinner.After tasting the Huamei Pork Ribs just now, he also had a little bit of expectation for the Dry Pot Sausage. Maybe it would also taste very good.With this idea in mind, he picked up the sausage. Before he put it into his mouth, the unique spicy aroma of the dry pot sausage filled his nose. He chewed it and his eyes widened in surprise.Most of the fat sausages I have eaten in the past have been completely removed by the store. Although the finished product is not greasy at all, it tastes like a chewy skin and is very bland.Today's sausage retains the fat inside, but it doesn't taste greasy at all. The seasonings are sufficient, and the flavor of chili, pepper and onion penetrates into every fold of the sausage. The outside of the sausage is soft and chewy. After chewing a few times, the fat inside melts in your mouth, and the flavors of various spices burst out in your mouth instantly.At this time, you have to eat a big mouthful of rice to feel satisfied.Bai Xiangning had prepared the rice before, and the plate with rice was just at his hand.The boss is really thoughtful.He filled a large bowl of rice and ate half of it in the blink of an eye.Next to him, Zhao Panyang has always been averse to animal offal foods, especially fatty intestines. He had eaten them once before, and he was almost vomited by the smell.Although people who like to eat fat sausage say that they eat it because of its unique taste, Zhao Panyang really can't accept it.But seeing Fang Wenjun eating so deliciously, he was a little moved.This time the sausage didn't seem to be smelly at all, it only smelled spicy and spicy.Just when he was hesitating, Fang Wenjun put several more sausages into the bowl, and even the second bowl of rice was filled.

Can't hesitate anymoreZhao Panyang picked up a piece of sausage, then put the sausage into his mouth with an expression as if he was facing an enemy.The spicy taste of the sausage stimulated Zhao Panyang's taste buds, and he couldn't help but start chewing.The more you chew, the more fragrant it becomes, and you can taste the rich aroma of oil every time you chew.The fat sausage has been processed so that there is no odor at all. The outer skin has been dry-fried and becomes crispy and fragrant, while the inner wall is plump and oily. Every inch of fat seems to be full of flavor, and every bite can surprise the taste buds.At this moment, Zhao Panyang felt that this grated pork intestine was so delicious that it was glowingNot only did it break his previous prejudice against fat intestines, but it also allowed him to see that someone could make an ingredient like fat intestines so delicious.He couldn't help but cast an admiring look at Bai Xiangning.Then I found that Fang Wenjun next to me was also looking at Boss Bai with special admiration.Fang Wenjun ate at least half of the plate of dry pot sausages just now. There are several people like Zhao Panyang who don't dare to eat fatty intestines. By the time they reacted and wanted to try it, the plates were empty.Since graduation, Fang Wenjun has never eaten the sausage that he likes, but the sausage made by Boss Bai today tastes even better than the one next to his school.The dish of fat intestines is simply cooked to perfection, unrivaled.As a loyal fan of Bai Xiangning, Chen Feng unconditionally believed in her cooking skills. He didn't hesitate at all from the moment the dishes were served, and every dish was poisoned by him.Before anyone could react, he ate all the dishes.After watching Zhao Panyang and Fang Wenjun compete for Huamei spareribs, Chen Feng was extremely grateful that he had just made the right decision.I was interested in this piece first, don't grab it from me.What you are interested in is that once you eat it in my mouth, it belongs to me.Hey, hey, leave some for meDon't pour that soup, I want to mix it with rice.It was a noisy meal, but the decoration team has always been on good terms with each other. Although they were fighting over the food this time, it was only a small quarrel and they didn't get red in the face.When they were almost finished eating, Bai Xiangning placed another small plate in front of everyone. In the center of the white porcelain plate was a crystal clear snack.This is bayberry jelly, dessert after the meal.Wow, there is even dessert after the meal.This dessert is so exquisite, like a ruby.Zhao Panyang held the edge of the porcelain plate and shook it gently, and the bayberry jelly placed on it also swayed from side to side, really like jelly.There is also a whole bayberry solidified on the top of the bayberry jelly. The change from deep red to light red makes this dessert look even better.Chen Feng took the lead in picking up the spoon, took a bite, and put the bayberry on it into his mouth. The unique sweet and sour taste of the bayberry immediately overflowed. I had just finished eating a large table of dishes, and my mouth was filled with the taste of meat. The bayberry jelly was sour and sweet, bringing a refreshing breath almost as soon as I took it into my mouth, dispelling the greasiness.The temperature of the mouth made the bayberry jelly melt immediately. Chen Feng tasted the bayberry. After a long time, he spit out a core.Once the bayberry jelly is finished, the meal truly ends. Everyone slumped on their chairs, looking satiated. When they looked at the dishes on the table, there were not even roots or leaves left.Seeing that they had finished eating, Bai Xiangning and Qiao Ping started to clear the table. Chen Feng immediately stood up and said proactively: Xiangning, let me help you.As soon as he finished speaking, Qiao Ping's hands seemed to move at twice the speed. She sent all the plates and bowls into the kitchen in one swipe, and then took the rag and wiped the table clean in three strokes.Chen Feng:Bai Xiangning was also stunned. Then when she saw that the tables had been cleared, she smiled and said to Chen Feng: It seems that there is no need to help.Qiao Ping stood aside. Although she lowered her head as usual, her back was straight and she felt inexplicably proud.Chen Feng felt that he could not be left behind. He racked his brains, and Zhao Panyang beside him suddenly said: Boss Bai, let me help you move the table back. I am strong and can move it easily.Before they came, Bai Xiangning and Qiao Ping moved the two tables together and put them together. They really put a lot of effort into it, so Bai Xiangning didn't shirk and said, "I'm sorry to bother you."Chen Feng quickly put the two tables back to their original positions with Zhao Panyang.After the meal, the decoration team and Bai Xiangning got to know each other quite well, so after eating, they started chatting with Bai Xiangning.Boss Bai, I'm so satisfied with today's meal. It's enough to satisfy my cravings.Another person chimed in bluntly: "Compared with today's meal, what did we eat at dinner parties before"Ahem, Chen Feng was embarrassed. After all, he had basically chosen the previous stores.But then I thought about it, wasn't he the one who chose today's store If it weren't for him, how would the decoration team have the chance to eat such delicious foodWhen he thought of this, he no longer felt guilty, but instead puffed up his chest, as if others were praising him for his discerning eyes.But after waiting for a long time, all I heard was praise and flattery for Bai Xiangning.In order to show his presence, Chen Feng took the initiative to find a new topic.By the way, Xiang Ning, when are you going to decorate the second floor

Chapter 11Wang Yalei was sitting on the bed in the dormitory, turning on the black box with his roommate, and fanning himself hard with a small fan, still complaining all the time.Our school is really stingy. It's such a hot day and there's power rationing. I'm almost dying of heat.Wang Yalei studied at T University, which is the best university in Jinghua City. The annual admission score is frighteningly high. He was admitted with the top 100 scores in the province.As long as you get into T University, you basically don't have to worry about finding a job after graduation.As a student of the software engineering department, he has become a hot prospect in the job market after graduation, and is the target of competition for countless large companies.T University is good at everything. It needs to be famous and famous, and it needs to be strong and capable.The school is just too stingy.With so many alumni sponsoring the school every year, they are still reluctant to turn on the air conditioning for the students all day long. Instead, they provide electricity for limited periods of time, in the name of training the students' hard-working spirit.Nonsence.The brothers' school next door laughed at them every day.Every time a T student proudly says: Our T University leads the country in scientific research and has countless famous alumni.University A next door would interrupt them coldly: But our air conditioner has no power limit.Student T: Our faculty is strong, with 12 academicians, 55 doctoral supervisors, andA: But we can turn on the air conditioner at will.T college students went berserk: Our school's ranking is higher than yoursBig A: Oh. But our air conditioner has no power limit.T college student:Break up.There is really nothing to talk about today.The roommate gnawed on the boneless chicken feet he had just bought from the school canteen and said vaguely: Well, I am so hot that I have no appetite to eat.Then what are you doing now Wang Yalei rolled his eyes at him. Even though this was his third pack of chicken feet, he still had the nerve to say that he couldn't eat anything.Zhang Xing held up the half-eaten chicken feet and argued: This is spicy and sour, appetizing.Just when Wang Yalei finished playing the game and looked at Victory on the computer screen, he threw the mouse on the bed and fell back.My stomach was already protesting from hunger, but my mouth just didn't want to eat anything.He looked at the time and saw that there was still an hour before the air conditioner could be turned on.At this time, the dormitory group shook wildly.breaking newsBai's Little Restaurant has new dishesThen a photo of the menu popped up: Today's Newspeak Plum Spare Ribs is NT$58/Three Cups of Chicken is NT$48.Finally, there is a seasonal limited dessert, bayberry jelly, 8 yuan.The person who sent the message was another person in the dormitory, nicknamed ADHD. Even on such a hot day, he was not idle. At this moment, he was reporting to his roommates in front of the Bai family restaurant.Wang Yalei suddenly stood up from the bed.What's going on Just looking at the menu, my appetite was aroused, and I immediately want to go to the store to eat the new products.He was just about to type when a new message popped up in the group: Hurry, hurry up, order all the new dishes, I'll be there soonIt was Zhang Xingfa who just had chicken feet in his mouth.Another roommate who was still studying for elective courses outside also followed closely and said, "I love this dish of three-cup chicken so much. Wait for me. I will skip Lao Zhao's class now to eat it."Very good, it seems that everyone in the dormitory has reached a consensus and decided to go to the Bai family restaurant for dinner.Wang Yalei and Zhang Xing put on their shoes, and their phones vibrated twice more. When they opened them, ADHD sent a message: Dad has taken a seat and ordered food. Come on, sons.Wang Yalei and Zhang Xing immediately swiped a long list of middle fingers.jpg underneath.When they arrived, Qiao Ping was just bringing the dishes to the table.When Bai Xiangning was in the kitchen, she specially arranged the ribs on a plate. The ribs of the same size were stacked in a pyramid shape, and the plum blossoms were scattered among them like decorations.The three-cup chicken is placed in a casserole with a wooden pot underneath. When it was served to the table, the soup inside was still bubbling. The fragrance emitted extremely quickly under this extremely high temperature, almost bursting out as soon as the lid was opened.So, so fragrantThey swallowed involuntarily.You can already imagine how delicious this dish isQiao Ping stood aside and reminded: The three-cup chicken has just come out of the pot, be careful to scald it.Seeing that these young men were all focused on the dishes and didn't seem to hear her at all, Qiao Ping smiled and went to greet other guests at the table.Began to eatI don't know who shouted first, and in the blink of an eye, half of the ribs on the plate were missing.When my tongue touches the sweet and sour sauce hanging on the ribs, my languorous appetite suddenly revives.Paihu roars Zhang Xing just stuffed two pieces of pork ribs and several plums into his mouth at once. At this time, his cheeks were bulging and he couldn't speak clearly.ADHD looked at him with contempt, he was really a pig eating ginseng fruit.Huh, don't eat it. Zhang Xing swallowed the food in his mouth and choked it back.Wang Yalei did not participate in the quarrel between the two of them, but concentrated on tasting the food.These ribs taste so tender. Once you taste them, you can tell they are fresh ribs, not the kind of inferior meat that has been frozen for who knows how long.Qiao Ping, who happened to be passing by, said: Our ingredients are purchased from the vegetable market every morning, and they are absolutely fresh.She has worked in the store for a while and knows that Bai Xiangning attaches great importance to the quality of ingredients.The raw material of this dish is pork ribs, and in order to ensure the quality of the finished dish, Bai Xiangning also uses the pure rib part in the middle of the ribs, where the meat is the most tender and full of flavor.The slightly older meaty parts on both sides were used by Bai Xiangning to make soup stock, making the best use of them and not wasting them.Although this will lead to an increase in costs, the quality of the finished dishes will be greatly improved.The pure ribs of the same size have been cooked for a long time and have a very uniform taste.After one bite, the full gravy explodes in your mouth, blending with the sweet and sour sauce wrapped around it, as if dancing together in your mouth, the combination is very harmonious.Oh my God, how did the boss prepare this sauce It's so special and delicious.Yes, there are some stores out there that use tomato sauce to make sweet and sour sauce, and the resulting pork ribs have an indescribable taste. I have stepped on this mistake countless times before.That's it, do these unscrupulous restaurants think that customers can't tell the difference I'll never go there again after eating it once.Although this dish is called Plum Spare Ribs, it is actually just a slight change from the Sweet and Sour Spare Ribs, and the general method is the same.The addition of plums gives this dish a richer taste and layer, and you will feel a refreshing fragrance of plums when you eat it.The entire dish was cooked without adding a drop of soy sauce. The bright red sauce hanging on the ribs completely benefited from the sugar color that Bai Xiangning carefully brewed.Stir-frying the color of sugar is a technical job. If it is not stir-fried properly, the color will not be rosy and bright, and if it is over-stirred, the finished dish will become bitter.The Baixiang Ning is cooked to the right sugary color. After the ribs are served, the attractive color will whet your appetite almost instantly.Wang Yalei picked up another piece of ribs, and his teeth could easily come off the bone without using too much force. The rich sauce fills every inch of the ribs, and with one bite, the meat juice fills the entire mouth.Occasionally, I will eat one or two plums, which are sour and give people a surprise that is different from the spareribs.Just when they were intoxicated with the deliciousness of Huamei Spare Ribs, there was a howl of ghosts and wolves next to them.Ah ah ah why didn't you wait for meTurning around, he saw He Peng, who was forgotten in the corner by them and was taking elective courses.He Peng continued to wail, you heartless dogs have already eaten all the ribs, do you want me to lick the plateHe sat down and pretended to wipe away his tears, pitying me for skipping class after all my hard work.Wang Yalei said: Wouldn't it be nice to order another plateIt just so happened that they didn't eat enough either.Although the portions of the dishes are large, they are still growing young men and must eat enough.He Peng waved to Bai Xiangning excitedly.Boss, here's another one: Plum Pork Ribs

Chapter 12Everyone except He Peng had just eaten a lot of pork ribs, so when He Peng picked up several pieces of three-cup chicken at once, they didn't say anything. After all, He Peng's favorite three-cup chicken was the whole one. Things everyone in the dormitory knows.As soon as He Peng took the first bite, his eyes immediately lit up. The disappointment of not eating plum pork ribs was immediately diluted. Now there are only two words playing in his brain.delicious yummy yummyHe never thought that the three-cup chicken could be so delicious. Compared with this time, the three-cup chicken he had eaten before was simply a younger brother.The other three people couldn't resist the strong aroma of three cups of chicken, so they all picked up chicken pieces and put them in their mouths.Wow, it's so delicious. The chicken is so tender.With a gentle pinch of the chopsticks, the chicken pieces were separated from the bones. After

Zhang Xing finished eating the chicken, he even crunched the bones. This dish is so delicious that even the seams between the bones seem to be soaked with soup. With a slight sip, the thick sauce flows into your mouth.Three cups of chicken, what is three cupsJust use a cup of rice wine, a cup of sesame oil, and a cup of soy sauce, and you can cook it without adding a drop of water.It is best to use a casserole to make this dish. Cover it with a lid and simmer it over low heat. The heat is compressed in this small space. The flavor of the three cups of seasonings penetrates into the chicken. Finally, the juice is reduced over high heat, and the chicken becomes dark brown. The mellow sauce is firmly coated on the chicken pieces, tempting anyone who sees it to taste it.The casserole is kept warm. The chicken pieces are still a little hot and need to be blown twice before you can eat them. When the chopsticks pick up the chicken pieces from the casserole, the thick sauce seems to cover the chicken with a thick, shiny film, slowly dripping onto the white and crystal clear rice.Eating a bite of rice with the sauce is an incomparable feeling of satisfaction.Different from the sweet and sour taste of the plum pork ribs just now, the three-cup chicken tastes salty and fresh. When you taste it again, you can taste a hint of sweetness. The seemingly non-existent sweetness makes the whole dish even more delicious. One floor.When you take a bite, the salty, fresh, sweet and soy flavors are intertwined. It is a delicious food that is indescribable in any words.It's amazing, except for the chicken legs, why the meat of other parts is so tenderWang Yalei, who didn't get the chicken legs but was chewing the chicken breasts, agreed: It's true, even the chicken breasts I'm eating now are not bad at all and don't fill my teeth at all.ADHD took a few spoonfuls of the soup from the casserole and poured it over the rice. The brown-red oily sauce slowly penetrated and the rice grains were dyed an attractive brown-red color.Ouch, ow, ow, that's great.The soup is condensed with the deliciousness of chicken, and blended with the flavor of sesame oil, rice wine, and soy sauce. It can be mixed with rice and eaten in several large bowls.When the three cups of chicken were almost finished, the second plate of plum pork ribs they ordered was also served.Only then did He Peng see the whole picture of Huamei Spare Ribs. Each piece of the neatly stacked ribs was evenly coated with bright red sauce, and even glowed under the light.He tasted a piece, and the meat juices that had been tightly locked inside suddenly surged out. The plump meat juice seemed to have no end. Every time he chewed, more juice would rush out from the gaps in the ribs, and then dominate his mouth.The second plate of plum pork ribs didn't stay on the table for too long, and then it all went into the stomachs of the four people in the dormitory.As soon as they put down their chopsticks, Qiao Ping came over in time and placed a small plate in front of everyone.There is bayberry jelly in the center of the plate, which is soft and tender, with a clear red color, and a whole bayberry is placed on the top.This is iced bayberry jelly, please use it slowly.The four people who were slumped on the chairs immediately stood up.Oops, I almost forgot that I also ordered bayberry jellyIt looks so exquisite. Try it now.This bayberry jelly must have just been taken out of the refrigerator. Take a spoonful and taste it, and the refreshing sweet and sour coolness will immediately sweep through your mouth.Just now, the plum was an appetizer, but the bayberry at this time was to relieve fatigue. They were both plums, but they had completely different effects.After all the bayberry jelly was eaten, the meal was completely finished.Burping is easyThis meal is so satisfyingThere were four people in the dormitory, and everyone ate at least three large bowls of rice, even the three cups of chicken soup in the casserole, and ate them together with the rice.Operation CD, they practiced it very well.Let's come here for dinner from now on.That's necessary. If possible, I want to have dinner together every day, heheheAt this time, some people started to make trouble. Today I broke the rules and actually ate four bowls of rice. How many steps do I have to run to burn off these caloriesADHD, who was still clamoring for fitness two days ago, began to feel regretful.Then I won't call you next time I come here to eat.noJust at this time, Bai Xiangning passed by, ADHD immediately said to Bai Xiangning: Boss Bai, this new dish is so delicious.Bai Xiangning stopped and said with a smile:

You can eat as much as you like. There will be more new dishes later, so please come and support them.The four people said in unison: That is necessary.Originally, dry-pot sausages were also on Bai Xiangning's new menu, but cleaning fresh sausages is troublesome and requires repeated cleaning to remove the odor inside the sausages.If this dish is served, it will take a lot of time just to prepare it. Currently, there are only two people in the store, she and Qiao Ping, and the supply of other dishes cannot be guaranteed.Moreover, some people could not accept the taste of fat intestines as animal offal, so she later replaced the dry pot fat intestines with the more widely accepted three-cup chicken.She looked around the store, and most of the customers had this dish on their tables. Now it seemed that the decision she made at that time was indeed the right one.ADHD chose the largest table in the restaurant, but it could only seat four people. Originally, Bai Xiangning launched rice bowls in the form of fast food, ready to eat and go, so no one would choose to have a meal here.Zhang Xing looked at the seats around him that were already full and said: Fortunately, we came early.It would be great if Bai's Little Restaurant expanded its store. Wang Yalei also said that business is so booming now that there is simply not enough space in the store to sit.Yes, it's best to get a private room so that we can have dinner together later.Hey, hey, when I came here today, I thought I heard Boss Bai say that the second floor is already being renovated. It will probably be installed in a few days.real or fakeit is true. A soft female voice that was different from theirs sounded. They turned around and saw that it was Bai Xiangning.She had just come from another table and happened to hear them discussing this matter when passing by, so she gave them a positive reply.Two private rooms have been set up on the second floor, and a few more tables have been added. According to the current progress, in a few days, everyone will be able to eat on the second floor.Last time Chen Feng and the others came to dinner, they mentioned the decoration of the second floor. This coincided with Bai Xiangning's idea, so she took advantage of the situation and finalized the matter.The small restaurant is now developing well, and the customer flow in the store is increasing day by day. Only the first floor can no longer meet the needs of customers.Recently, many customers have been asking about the possibility of expanding the store or opening a branch.Opening a branch is currently out of the question because the funds required far exceed what she currently has, and the lack of manpower is also a huge problem, so she can only consider it later. But to expand the store, you only need to use the space on the second floor.It turns out that the second floor was Bai Xiangning's living room. Since it needs to be renovated, she definitely can't continue to live on the second floor.Behind the snack street is an old-fashioned residential building, so she rented a one-bedroom apartment in the community for 800 a month, which was not expensive.The most important thing is that it is very close to a small restaurant, just a few minutes' walk away.The small restaurant only opens in the evening, and the decoration team works from morning to four in the afternoon, so as not to affect the normal business of the small restaurant.Chen Feng and the others happened to have no other projects during this time, so everyone was mobilized and the construction speed was much faster.The second floor was partitioned to create two separate spaces. According to Bai Xiangning's idea, there are two private rooms, one large and one small. The larger one can accommodate eight to ten people, while the smaller one can accommodate four to six people.Two sizes of private rooms can meet the needs of different customer groups.The progress is now over half, and the decoration on the second floor will be completed in a few days.Boss Bai, since the second floor will be decorated in a few days, can we reserve a private room nowWang Yalei said.

Chapter 13Why can I reserve a private room nowBoss, I also want to make an appointmentI want to make an appointment with my boss next Monday night. Be sure to leave me a private room.As soon as Wang Yalei finished speaking, the surrounding guests who had been concentrating on eating seemed to be in a panic. They all stood up and crowded around Bai Xiangning, for fear that they would not be able to grab a seat in the box if they were too late.For a moment, the sound of chairs mopping the floor, clinking bowls and chopsticks, and people shouting mixed together, making it very noisy.The other three people in the dormitory had a tacit understanding. They all looked at Wang Yalei in silence, their eyes almost killing him.Wang Yalei:The voice I just spoke was obviously not loud. He even lowered his voice to avoid attracting attention.He was on the verge of tears right now. He originally wanted to take advantage of the fact that not many people knew the news and quickly book a private room, but in the end, he attracted all the people around him.This group of people were eating without raising their heads just nowWho pays attention to what the people next to them are saying when eatingThe table where Wang Yalei and his group were eating was crooked by the crowds around them. If they hadn't used their feet to hold it up, the table would have been pushed to nowhere.Everyone please calm down.Bai Xiangning obviously did not expect that the situation would suddenly turn into this. She really underestimated the enthusiasm of the guests. The private rooms were not even installed, but there were so many people wanting to make reservations.In this chaotic situation, Bai Xiangning, as the boss, can only stabilize the situation.Everyone listen to meShe raised her hands and pressed them down slightly toward the crowd, signaling the guests to be quiet.The noisy voice suddenly dropped, and the guests were waiting for Bai Xiangning to speak.Thank you very much for your love. The second floor is currently under renovation, and the two newly established private rooms are temporarily unavailable. Bai Xiangning first reported to everyone the progress of the decoration on the second floor. According to the current speed, the second floor will be completed in four or five days. Reservations will not open until the second floor is fully renovated, so please be patient.Ah, so now I can't make a reservation and some customers will be unhappy.Boss Bai, please open reservations now. Our whole family happens to be here. Just give us a private room for any day next week. The speaker was a young man.An aunt standing next to him immediately said: Hey, you young man, why are you like this Why does Boss Bai have to reserve a seat for you If he does, it will also be reserved for us elderly people.What's wrong with getting older I still have a one- or two-year-old baby at home.Seeing these people quarreling again, Bai Xiangning felt dizzy.Everyone, I will set up a group. If you have anything to say in the group, okayOkay, boss, please join a group. If we want to make an appointment in the future, we can tell you in the group.As soon as they heard that Bai Xiangning wanted to join the group, everyone who had been noisy just now lowered their heads and opened WeChat. As soon as Bai Xiangning gave the order, they immediately scanned the QR code and rushed into the group.Because there were so many people, a representative from each family was invited to join the group first, and then the family members were invited in.This is much faster than Bai Xiangning pulling people one by one, but there are still many people who did not join the group.Bai Xiangning called Qiao Ping over, "Qiao Ping, go and print out the group QR code and stick it at the door so that anyone who comes in later can see it."OK, I'll be right back.Qiao Ping squeezed out of the crowd, jogged all the way to the printing shop in front to print out the QR code, and then ran back without any delay. The trip took less than five minutes.Huh, huh. Qiao Ping stood panting at the door. Before she could catch her breath, she hurriedly posted the paper with the QR code printed on it in the most conspicuous place at the door of the store.Anyone who enters the store can see it at a glance.Husband, please walk faster, stop looking at your phone, wait until we finish eating.Yu Xin walked to the small restaurant with her husband and son as soon as she got off work. They also heard that the small restaurant had new dishes. They happened to have time today and wanted to come over and try them.When he was almost there, Yu Xin said in surprise: Why are there so many people queuing in front of the small restaurantHe Kang'an immediately pulled his son and followed him. There was a crowd inside and outside the small restaurant, and people were crowded together.What day is it today Why are there so many peopleYu Xin couldn't help complaining: It's all your fault for wasting time just now.

There are so many people, how long do we have to wait in lineHe Kang'an touched his nose and felt a little guilty. He just lowered his head and looked at his phone for a moment. Who knew when he looked up, there were so many people in the small restaurant.Let's go over first and see what's going on.Although the business of the small restaurant is good, it has never seen a scene like today, so I'd better go and see it first.The family of three quickened their pace and walked to the door of the small restaurant. They immediately saw the QR code posted outside. There was a line of large black characters on the top: Bai Family Small Restaurant Customer Group.Yu Xin and He Kangan scanned the QR code respectively, and after entering, they found that there were already hundreds of people in the group.A large part of the crowded crowd had already finished their meal. They left after entering the group, otherwise they would have been stuck here and delayed the boss's business.The originally crowded small restaurant suddenly became much empty, and Yu Xin and He Kangan found a seat to sit down.It's good for the boss to create a group. If there is any news in the future, you can notify it in the group.He Kang'an strongly agrees with his wife's view. Yes, for example, when new dishes will be served, what new dishes are served, and what the prices are, all can be announced in the group in advance. How convenient for everyone.Well, let's discuss this later. Let's order the dishes first. Yu Xin has been very busy these days. She usually asks her husband to pack food for her when she wants to eat in a small restaurant. She hasn't come to a restaurant for a long time. Today she finally has the opportunity to come over. She wants to order all the new dishes in the restaurant. Again.You guys are here. I haven't seen you for a long time.Yu Xin's family are old customers who have been patronizing the small restaurant since it opened. Seeing them coming, Bai Xiangning went to say hello.Yes, I was working overtime a while ago, and I almost wanted to eat in a small restaurant. It was rare that I was free today, so I rushed over immediately.Bai Xiangning said with a smile: "Then wait a moment, the food will be here soon."After all the dishes were served, Yu Xin couldn't wait to pick up her chopsticks and start eating. He Kang'an and He Tongtong were not willing to lag behind and joined the battle one after another.Within a moment, the three of them had swept away the food.After Yu Xin finished eating, she quickly returned to her elegant posture. She slowly wiped her mouth with a tissue, and then said: It's so delicious, so satisfying, I'm so happy.Although her husband often packed food from small restaurants for her before, the food she packed was definitely not as good as what she ate in the store.When the three cups of chicken were first served, the thick soup was still boiling, not to mention how fragrant it was. There is also the plum pork ribs. The pork ribs are tender and delicious. The sweet and sour taste of plums penetrates into the ribs, and the delicious taste of the ribs seems to have penetrated into the plums. The flavors of the two blend with each other and match perfectly.He Tongtong pursed his lips, Mom and Dad, you just ate so many ribs that he couldn't grab them, so he could only eat a little pitiful plum like this.Yu Xin immediately put on a straight face, pointed at the bones at He Tongtong's hand and said: Count how much you have eaten.ahHe Tongtong quickly destroyed the evidence and threw the cleanly chewed bones into the trash can. Then he looked at his mother innocently and said: I didn't eat any of them.Yu Xin: This little kid is getting more and more cunning.At this time, the crowd in the store had basically dispersed, and Bai Xiangning was finally able to breathe.Wang Yalei walked up to her and whispered: Boss Bai, I'm sorry, it's all up to me today. Although he didn't mean it, if he hadn't mentioned the reservation in the store, the situation wouldn't have become so confusing.Bai Xiangning saw the self-blame on his face and the whole person was wilted, so she said: "I don't blame you, it's because I didn't make arrangements in advance."Wow, Boss Bai is so kind. Not only did he not complain about him, he actually comforted him.He is a kindhearted person and his cooking is delicious. Boss Bai is the best person in the world.The little man crying in Wang Yalei's heart suddenly stopped feeling sad.In fact, Bai Xiangning told the truth. The main responsibility for today's situation does lie with her. She has been busy decorating during this period, but she didn't think much about what happened after the decoration.After the box is decorated, how to make a reservation is a problem.Although the group was created today, she just checked and found that the number of people in the group is now almost over a thousand. The number of guests has increased rapidly.There are so many people in the group, and there are always 99+ messages. If she makes an appointment in the group, there are so many messages, and she reads them one by one, which not only wastes time, but also easily misses the messages.Qiao Ping told her before that she could let customers add her on WeChat to make reservations. She had actually considered this method, but after thinking about it, she still felt it had disadvantages.She is usually busy with the business in the store most of the time. If too many people add her, she will not be able to reply in time.Boss Bai, are you thinking about how to make an appointmentSeeing Bai Xiangning looking worried, Wang Yalei guessed that it was most likely because of what happened just now.yes.Bai Xiangning told Wang Yalei her concerns.Wang Yalei is also a regular customer of the store. Bai Xiangning knew that he was a student of the Software Engineering Department of T University, so she wanted to ask him if there was any software that could realize the reservation function. After all, many softwares now have very powerful functions and can be used In all walks of life.When Wang Yalei heard this, he thought it was a coincidence that he had never found a suitable direction for his graduation practice, so when his other roommates started to build the framework, he had not even thought about the practical topic.As prospective graduates of T University's Software Engineering Department, the school's graduation requirement is that they personally develop a piece of software. As for what type of software, the school does not make too many requirements to limit the students' performance.And now, Wang Yalei decided that he would develop a unique software for Baijia Restaurant

Chapter 14Boss Bai, leave the software to me. I will make a software specifically for small restaurants. If you have any functions that need to be implemented, you can tell me.You said you wanted to make me a softwareyesBai Xiangning showed hesitation. She understood that Wang Yalei had good intentions, but she also knew that it was not easy to develop a software. It was a bit too much to bother him to make a software just because he made a reservation for a private room. Making a fuss out of a molehill.Boss Bai, you don't have to be mentally burdened. Developing a software is actually our graduation practice requirement, and it's not all for small restaurants. Seeing Bai Xiangning's hesitation, Wang Yalei explained again.Boss Bai, if I can't make this software for the small restaurant, I won't be able to graduate. Boss Bai, you are so kind, you shouldn't bear to see me kicked out of the house and living on the street because I can't graduate smoothly.Okay, okay, I agree.Wang Yalei suddenly beamed.Boss Bai, don't worry, I will be able to make the software soon and will definitely not delay your business.After saying this, Wang Yalei returned to school without stopping for a moment.On Tuesday night, a few people in the dormitory were playing games and eating late-night snacks. Only Wang Yalei had the curtains tightly drawn, so he didn't know what he was doing inside.Lei Zi, do you want to play black You are the only one missing.If you don't want to play, you can play by yourself. Wang Yalei's ruthless voice came from behind the curtain.If you really don't want to play, the jungle position has been reserved for you.Wang Yalei didn't reply directly.So several other people in the dormitory gathered together and whispered, Hey, have you noticed that Lei Zi has been acting strange recently He seems to be possessed by a demon. He doesn't play games or sleep. He just sits there every day and doesn't know what he is doing. .ADHD glanced at Wang Yalei's bed. Do you think he won't do anything bad behind our backWowWang Yalei suddenly opened the blackout curtain, what are you making up for me Who is doing something bad insideOuch, that's scaryThe black spots under Wang Yalei's eyelids were the result of staying up late for many days in a row. After working hard day and night for the past few days, he finally made the softwareHe debugged it many times, and now the software can basically run smoothly.Wang Yalei added Bai

Xiangning's WeChat account that day. After the software was completed, he couldn't wait to send a message to Bai Xiangning.But after waiting for a while, he didn't receive a reply. He looked at the time and saw that it was dinner time, so Boss Bai might not have time to look at his phone.He touched his empty stomach. He happened to be hungry, so he should go to the store to have a meal and talk to Boss Bai about this in person.No matter when I come to the small restaurant, the seats are always packed, including couples, parents with their children, and older couples.Bai Xiangning, wearing white work clothes, shuttled between tables.It was busy at this time, and Qiao Ping couldn't greet her outside alone, so after Bai Xiangning cooked the dishes, she would deliver them to the guests' tables.After serving the dishes for the last table of guests, Bai Xiangning leaned on the counter and rested for a while.Wang Yalei walked over and whispered to her excitedly: Boss Bai, the software is ready.With the lesson learned last time, Wang Yalei deliberately leaned into Bai Xiangning's ear this time, and also paid attention to the surroundings from time to time, for fear that others would hear him and cause commotion again.Bai Xiangning downloaded the software to her mobile phone according to his instructions. The software icon was orange, and the pattern on it was a large pot on a strong fire. There was a spatula inside, and it seemed that something was being stir-fried.Well, she liked the icon very much, it was perfect for a small restaurant.After clicking on it, the interface inside is also very simple. The most important thing at present is the reservation function.Everyone can register an account and then make an appointment directly in the software. Wang Yalei demonstrated it to Bai Xiangning. "Boss Bai, you can set the available reservation date here. If the date is gray, it means that the reservation for that day is full."Wang Yalei's software interface guidance is very good, and Bai Xiangning roughly understands how to use this software after a simple operation.Boss Bai, the current function of the software is relatively simple. If you have new ideas later, you can tell me and I will optimize it at any time.When they make software, they are not done after developing the software. They also need to be responsible for the maintenance and update of the software in the future. The current demand of small restaurants is private room reservations, so the functions he developed are relatively simple. In the future, as small restaurants become larger and larger, they will definitely need more and more functions.Bai Xiangning became more and more satisfied with this software. Although it only had one function, it was enough. After all, her small restaurant didn't have that much business now.You haven't eaten yet. Whatever you want to eat today, you can order whatever you want. I'll treat you.Wow, Boss Bai, you are so nice. Wang Yalei was very surprised.Bai Xiangning said it very sincerely, not politely, so Wang Yalei did not shirk it, Boss Bai, I want to eat three cups of chicken and mapo tofu.Okay, just find a place to sit and wait. You'll be fine soon. Bai Xiangning said to him with a smile.Wang Yalei randomly found a seat by the window, then sat down and started scanning the restaurant's customer base. Every time I open it, the messages inside are 99+.I heard that the second floor of the small restaurant will be completed tomorrow. When can we reserve a private roomI also want to know that a few of my best friends who I haven＇t seen in many years are coming to Jinghua City. If I can get a private room this time, I plan to let them come to the small restaurant to experience our most delicious restaurant in Jinghua City.Next weekend is my old lady＇s 80th birthday. Since she last ate the Plum Pork Ribs that I packed back, she has been talking about it every day. Now when she sees me, I tell her to take her to the store to eat once. I hope it can make me happy. Grab a private room and fulfill the old man's wish.So how do I make a reservation for a private room now I＇m so anxious.Want to know +1Want to know +2

The group is like a relay race, with dozens of the same content being viewed at once.Wang Yalei really wanted to tell them how to make an appointment, but he still suppressed his desire to share.It would be better for Boss Bai to talk about this matter himself.Not long after, Bai Xiangning came out of the kitchen with two steaming dishes. Before she reached Wang Yalei, the aroma was already wafting over, and Wang Yalei's stomach growled twice in response.You're so hungry.

I'll serve you some more rice.After putting down the dishes, Bai Xiangning turned around and went to the kitchen to serve a large bowl of rice to Wang Yalei. At the end, she asked with concern: Is this enough If not, you can add more.Wang Yalei looked at the rice piled like a hill in front of him. Did Boss Bai regard him as a rice pail With so much rice, it would be more than enough for two people.Enough, enoughThen you eat slowly and I will talk about the software in the group.When Wang Yalei heard this, he immediately put down the chopsticks he was about to pick up. Boss Bai, are you planning to open reservations todayIf it were to open today, he should be able to grab a spot with his hand speed of playing games for many years. Thinking about it, his hand had already touched the phone, and as soon as she sent a message, he would immediately grab it.Bai Xiangning said: Yes, I just set it up and plan to open reservations for the next month.Wang Yalei unlocked his phone, the screen stayed on the group message interface, and then looked at Bai Xiangning with burning eyes.Bai Xiangning was amused by the way he was ready to go. You don't have to compete for a spot. You have the privilege to choose in advance.Really, reallyCan you really give me priority Wang Yalei was almost stunned by this sudden surprise.Bai Xiangning nodded and said: Is this still false You decide which day you want to come, and I will lock in the box quota for that day.Wang Yalei opened the calendar on his phone with trembling hands. His parents were coming to visit him this Saturday, so he booked a private room for this Saturday.His hometown is in the next province, and he usually only has the chance to go home during holidays. This time it happened to coincide with the Dragon Boat Festival, so his parents proposed to come to Jinghua City to see him.How many of you are there Bai Xiangning asked, because the private rooms were one large and one small, so she had to ask the number of people in advance.Three or four people.Okay, I'll leave a small box for you.Wang Yalei returned to the dormitory in a daze. He didn't expect that he could book a private room so easily. His happy dizziness lasted until he fell asleep.He had a sweet dream.At the same time, the fight for the box seats in the group is still going on.Wang Yalei, who was sleeping soundly, had no idea about this.

Chapter 15What kind of software is this I've never heard of it. It can't be phishing software.If her best friend hadn't been on a voice call with her at this moment, Xiao Qian would have suspected that her account had been hacked. Otherwise, how could she have let her register an account on a software she had never heard of before, and stayed up all night, forcing her to do so What's the quota for her to grab togetherSu Yutong stared at the phone screen with all her attention. When she heard her best friend's question, she said: Oh, just believe me this time. As long as you get the spot, I guarantee you will never regret it.However, the two refreshed the interface countless times, and the date they wanted to make an appointment was always gray.Xiao Qian was tired, so she put down her mobile phone, lying on her side on the pillow and said to Su Yutong on the other end of the phone: Isn't it just a private room in a hotel If you can't get a private room, can't you eat in the restaurantSu Yutong gritted her teeth. Damn it, she still lost because of her hand speed.Of course it's okay not to sit in the box, but she just wants to experience the feeling that she has that others don't have.Xiao Qian felt her depression. Although she felt that it was not a big deal, she still comforted her by saying: Don't take this matter to your heart. Anyway, I will come see you this week, and then we will go to other restaurants to eat.No, Su Yutong said without thinking.ahIf you didn't grab it, you didn't grab it. Then we have to go to a small restaurant to eat. Su Yutong muttered something. It doesn't matter. It's the same thing if you sit outside. The private room is not good at all, hum.Xiao Qian:Then why are you working so late at nightAfter the decoration on the second floor was completed, Bai Xiangning planned to invite Chen Feng and the rest of the decoration team to have a meal together to express her gratitude.However, after most of the decoration team finished decorating the small restaurant, they had to rush to the next city to work on the next project, so there was no way to have a dinner together.I owe you this meal now, and I'll wait for you to come over and eat it whenever you have time. Bai Xiangning said with a smile, tell me in advance that the big box will be reserved for you.Zhao Panyang said happily: Then we will remember it.Chen Feng did not leave with the large army. Uncle Chen had sprained his ankle some time ago and wanted to stay with his parents for a while.He is usually away from Jinghua City most of the time, and it is rare for him to have the opportunity to spend more time with his parents.So in the end, Bai Xiangning and Chen Feng's family had dinner together, and they chatted about their family affairs while eating.Sister Xiang Ning, thank you for sending my dad to the hospital in time last time. The doctor said that if he came later, he might have sequelae. I'm not here usually, but luckily I have you to help take care of me.Uncle Chen knocked his son on the head and said unhappily: Why do you make it look like your father can't take care of himself My legs and feet are flexible.Then why did you sprain your ankle last time Mrs. Chen mercilessly exposed his background.Uncle Chen has been stubborn all his life. He said harshly: I was walking well, but who knew that a stone suddenly jumped out in front of me and attacked meThat morning, Bai Xiangning was preparing ingredients in the kitchen when she suddenly heard a cry of pain from next door. She recognized that it was Uncle Chen's voice, so she quickly put down the half-cut vegetables and ran out to see what was going on. .I saw Uncle Chen sitting on the small bench, his face pinched together in pain.Grandma Chen was also panicked at the time and was so anxious that she didn't know what to do.When Bai Xiangning saw this, she immediately called 120. The ambulance came quickly and took Uncle Chen to the hospital.Uncle Chen is not young anymore. If a young person sprains his foot, it may take a while, but for an older person, it will be serious if he twists his foot even slightly.I didn't do anything, but for my neighbors, I don't need to take this little thing to heart.Bai Xiangning continued: "I usually take good care of you. If you hadn't helped me in the beginning, I would have starved to death, and there would be no small restaurant now. Speaking of which, I should thank you."Grandma Chen said angrily: Oh, you kid, why are you so polite to us You just said you don't need to take these little things to heart. We have been neighbors for so long, so isn't it normal to take care of each otherYou're right, I was the one who saw things differently. By the way, it's almost the Dragon Boat Festival. I made some rice dumplings today and brought them out for everyone to try.Bai Xiangning quickly brought a bamboo basket from the kitchen.Several other people were surprised when they saw the rice dumplings in the basket.Xiang Ning, is this a zongzi Why are they squareYes, these are rice dumplings.Uncle Chen picked up a square-shaped rice dumpling with novelty and said: This is the first time I have seen a rice dumpling with this shape. The wrapping of this rice dumpling is really unique. We at Xiang Ning are so skillful in making this rice dumpling look like a work of art. Grandma Chen also took one and put it in her hand, looking left and right. This is a dice rice dumpling. I had a sudden idea a few days ago, and then I tried to wrap the rice dumpling into a square shape. It looked like a dice, so I named it dice rice dumpling. This time I made candied date rice dumplings and salted egg yolk meat rice dumplings. Try them and see how they taste. The two kinds of rice dumplings she made this time were of relatively common flavors, mainly because she wanted to try this unique way of making rice dumplings. The rice dumplings were freshly cooked and were still steaming in the palm of your hand. The unique and fresh smell of the rice dumpling leaves curled up, arousing the greed in everyone's stomach. They picked up the rice dumplings and slowly peeled off the leaves. As the outer skin peeled off, the fragrant glutinous rice filling was exposed to everyone, and they could tell at a glance what the filling was inside. The glutinous rice wrapped with candied dates is shiny white, and the candied dates are like a deep red agate embedded in the center, making the surrounding glutinous rice dyed with a light red color. After taking a gentle bite, your teeth immediately fell into the gentle trap of the glutinous rice, making it difficult to extricate yourself. Bai Xiangning soaked the glutinous rice in sugar water one night in advance, so the cooked glutinous rice not only absorbed the aroma of the rice dumpling leaves, but also had a sweet taste, which was sticky and glutinous, sweet to the heart.The salted egg yolk meat rice dumplings are a little different. The glutinous rice is soaked in sauce in advance and becomes dark brown in color after cooking. The salted egg yolk almost completely blends into the surrounding glutinous rice, and the oil from the meat also penetrates into the glutinous rice, making it very satisfying to eat.Bai Xiangning cooked a total of eight rice dumplings, and they were all eaten in a short time. Only some rice dumpling leaves with glutinous rice were left in the bamboo basket.Xiang Ning, the rice dumplings you make are not only beautiful, but also delicious.Glutinous rice fills her stomach, so Grandma Chen rarely eats it. Originally, she only planned to eat one today, but the rice dumplings made by Baixiang Ning were so delicious that she couldn't hold back one, so she ate two, and she almost missed it. He snatched the one from Chen Feng's hand.Mom, if you eat too much glutinous rice and it's hard to digest, you can't eat it anymore. If Chen Feng hadn't tried his best to dissuade her, he would have lost the remaining candied date rice dumpling in his hand.Grandma Chen was still not satisfied. She smacked her lips and said: Who said glutinous rice is filling I ate two and I didn't feel anything in my stomach.

Chapter 16Xiao Qian and Su Yutong were college roommates. After graduation, they returned to their respective hometowns. They were not in the same city, but they were not far away. It only took more than an hour by high-speed rail.Xiao Qian bought a ticket for Friday night and arrived at Jinghua City at exactly eight o'clock. Su Yutong originally wanted to take Xiao Qian to the Bai Family Restaurant that night, but it was almost nine o'clock when Xiao Qian arrived at the station and took the bus to her house, and the restaurant had already closed by then.The two of them bought some food at the midnight snack stall. Xiao Qian didn't eat at night. Now she was so hungry that her chest pressed against her back. She held a bowl of cold skin and drank half of it in the blink of an eye. After eating, her hunger was relieved. A lot.Tongtong, where should we go to eat tomorrow I searched for guides before coming here, and I heard that there is a very famous hotpot restaurant nearby. Xiao Qian dug out the guide she had found before and pointed out the store to Su Yutong.No, no, I've been to this restaurant. It's disgusting. Su Yutong only glanced at it and shook her head. This restaurant relies entirely on marketing. Its main focus is to deceive one after another. There will be no repeat customers at all.Really, really Xiao Qian couldn't help but waver in her judgment. She thought she had chosen a good store, but she didn't expect that she was immediately dismissed by Su Yutong.Then you tell me where to eat, I will listen to you. Xiao Qian said.After all, Su Yutong has stayed in Jinghua City for so long, so she must know the food in Jinghua City better.Didn't I just say that last night, go eat at Bai's Little RestaurantAh, Xiao Qian looked embarrassed. She thought her best friend was just talking casually last night, but she actually went to eat at that little-known restaurant.In fact, when Su Yutong told her last night, she had searched the Internet, but she didn't find any useful information. It seemed like it was just a fly shop.Su Yutong immediately retorted: Who said it was a little-known restaurant After eating there, I couldn't stop thinking about it day and night.Xiao Qian was still hesitating, Su Yutong took her arm, oh, you still don't believe me, how have I ever tricked youOh well.Anyway, she has to stay in Jinghua City for two days. Even if the meal today is not delicious, the worst she can do is eat somewhere else tomorrow.Seeing Xiao Qian nodding, Su Yutong took her to the small restaurant. Hurry up, go early, otherwise there will be too many people waiting for you.Xiao Qian lowered her psychological expectations to a minimum, and then followed her best friend to a small restaurant.They arrived early and there were not many people in the store.Wow, it's new againThere are a few big words written on the small blackboard: candied date rice dumpling 5 yuan/piece, crystal rice dumpling 6 yuan/piece, egg yolk meat rice dumpling 7 yuan/piece.There are three bamboo baskets on the counter, each containing different flavors of rice dumplings.Is this a rice dumpling Xiao Qian noticed the unusual shape of the rice dumplings and was a little surprised. She had never seen rice dumplings wrapped like this before. Is this store doing a gimmickThe shape does look unique. Each rice dumpling is square and placed there like stacking blocks. It looks very neat. I just don't know what it will taste likeSu Yutong had a look of surprise on her face. Boss, there are two of these three flavors of rice dumplings.Hey, don't order so much, we may not be able to finish it. Xiao Qian tried to stop her, the rice dumplings are very filling.Oh, it's okay. If you can't finish it, just pack it back and it won't be wasted anyway.The rice dumplings were cooked in advance, so Qiao Ping quickly brought them the rice dumplings they ordered. Xiao Qian feels that this rice dumpling also has an advantage, that is, it is not as easy to stagger around as ordinary rice dumplings. The rice dumplings are placed on a rectangular porcelain plate, six neatly.Well, these rice dumplings smell quite fragrant.Xiao Qian's nostrils twitched, and the fragrance emanating from the rice dumplings slowly drifted into her nose. Only very fresh rice dumpling leaves can emit such a fresh and pleasant smell.She couldn't help but wonder what the zongzi tasted like.Which one tastes best to eat firstUh-huh, it's delicious. I want another one. Su Yutong was so forgetful about eating that she took another zongzi before she remembered Xiao Qian across from her. Hey, Qianqian, why haven't you eaten yetXiao Qian looked at the plate with only two rice dumplings left and felt that it was outrageous.Why didn't she know that her best friend had such a big appetite In such a short time, she actually ate four rice dumplings.Xiao Qian stopped worrying and took one of the remaining two rice dumplings. If she thought about it for a second longer, the plate would be completely empty.What she was holding was a meat rice dumpling. After peeling it off, Xiao Qian suddenly felt that the rice dumpling was really cute. It stood upright on the rice dumpling leaf like a small cube, as if nervously waiting for her to taste it. Just looking at it, she could imagine The sticky texture to the entrance.She took a bite and was pleasantly surprised.The glutinous rice is pressed very tightly, absorbing the aroma of pork belly fat, and is wrapped in the fragrance of rice dumpling leaves, making it delicious when eaten in the mouth. The salted egg yolk seems to melt into the glutinous rice, and the edges become a little sandy, but the inside is very dense and tastes extremely salty.The meat inside has been marinated in advance, making it crispy, glutinous and delicious. A bite of glutinous rice and a bite of meat brings an extremely wonderful experience to the taste buds.The rice dumplings are cooked just right and stick to your teeth slightly, but not too sticky. As you continue to chew, the aroma gradually fills your entire mouth.The last rice dumpling on the plate is a crystal rice dumpling. After peeling it off, the inside is translucent. Different from ordinary rice dumplings, crystal rice dumplings use sago instead of glutinous rice, so they are transparent when cooked. There are some raisins in it, which tastes chewy and delicious, with a hint of sweetness.Just now Xiao Qian was worried that they wouldn't be able to finish the meal, but in less than ten minutes, all six rice dumplings were eaten, leaving only scattered rice dumpling leaves on the plate.Su Yutong ate four rice dumplings at once, and her stomach was a little full no matter how big it was. She kept rubbing her belly. When Xiao Qian saw it, she thought she ate too fast and had an upset stomach.Are you OKIt's okay, I'm just promoting intestinal digestion. After all, I'm not satisfied yet. I have to order some other dishes later.Just kidding, Xiao Qian finally came to Jinghua City. How could she just take her to eat rice dumplings She also had to eat all the dishes in the small restaurant.She wanted to fulfill her duties as a landlord, and Su Yutong found a reason for herself.It's not that she wants to eat it.ahWhat's wrong Xiao Qian was startled by Su Yutong's surprise. She thought something had happened to her. Unexpectedly, Su Yutong covered her face and said regretfully: I just ate in a hurry and forgot to take a photo.Xiao Qian: She thought it was a big deal.I'll order some more rice dumplings. Xiao Qian said.She hadn't eaten the candied date rice dumplings just now, so she wanted to try them.The two ordered rice dumplings of each flavor again. This time, Su Yutong did not rush to eat. Instead, she took out her mobile phone and took many photos of the dice rice dumplings from different angles. Some were taken separately and some were taken together. Yes, click, click, click, I took a dozen pictures at once.Well, this one is pretty good, and so is this one. Oops, I think that one is pretty cute too, so I'll stick with this one. Su Yutong fiddled with her cell phone and muttered something.Xiao Qian ate all the three rice dumplings she just ordered. Now it was better. She also ate one more than Su Yutong. So she also imitated Su Yutong and started rubbing her belly, hoping to digest it quickly.Although she hasn't eaten other dishes yet, the rice dumplings alone have made Xiao Qian's impression of this restaurant rise several levels.This rice dumpling is not only exquisite in appearance, but also tastes good. It can even be said to kill most of the rice dumplings she has eaten in an instant.When she was in school, she lived with her parents. Every year during the Dragon Boat Festival, her mother would take her to buy fresh rice dumpling leaves and then come back to make rice dumplings for her to eat.When Xiao Qian held the rice dumplings in her hands today, the familiar smell immediately reminded her of the Dragon Boat Festival when she was a child.Now she works in another city, and the round trip takes a day. She can only go back when she takes a long vacation.Just give them a call later. Xiao Qian thought.Ask your mother if she has made rice dumplings this year.

Chapter 17Phew, I feel like I can do it againSu Yutong

and Xiao Qian ordered the dishes first, and then walked around outside several times while waiting for the dishes. Finally, their stomachs were a little empty and they could make room for their next dishes.The food has just arrived. Let's go in quickly.Su Yutong kept her promise and actually ordered all the dishes available in the small restaurant. This time, Xiao Qian didn't stop Su Yutong because she was worried about not being able to finish the meal. A few dishes were nothing to them.On the table were mapo tofu, plum pork ribs, three-cup chicken and bayberry jelly.The two of them reached for the ribs with their chopsticks, then looked at each other and started to eat happily.When Xiao Qian took the first bite, she couldn't help but exclaimed: "How are these ribs made The meat is so tender and tastes sour and sweet. It's so appetizing."Su Yutong buried her head in eating. After hearing Xiao Qian's words, she took the time to reply: Let me just say that this restaurant is delicious. If you try other dishes, you will definitely not be disappointed.Hmm hmmAfter Xiao Qian finished eating one rib, she picked up a piece of three-cup chicken. The chicken pieces were covered in thick sauce, which smelled tempting and tasted delicious.This chicken is so delicious, the soup seems to seep into the bones, and the chicken is very fresh and delicious. Every dish surprises Xiao Qian. The food in this restaurant is really good.After the meal, their bellies were full.They ate rice dumplings first, and then ordered dishes. By the time they finished eating, it was almost eight o'clock in the evening, and there were many fewer people in the store.Bai Xiangning is not as busy as before, and she is wiping the counter when she has some free time.Su Yutong remembered the exquisitely shaped rice dumplings she had just eaten, so she walked to Bai Xiangning and asked curiously: Boss, your rice dumplings are so special. They are different from those I have seen before. How can you wrap them into a square shapeBai Xiangning thought for a while, and there happened to be some rice dumpling leaves left in the kitchen, so she said: I just have nothing to do now, so I will pack one for you to see.Wow, Wow, Wow, I want to see it. Su Yutong originally just asked casually, but she didn't expect that the boss was willing to demonstrate it to her in person. She waved to Xiao Qian excitedly, "Qianqian, come on, come on, come on, the boss will make rice dumplings on the spot."Her voice was loud, and not only did she attract Xiao Qian, but the other customers in the store also looked here curiously. A few who were about to leave after finishing their meal also turned around and walked towards the counter.In the blink of an eye, several people gathered next to the counter, all sticking their heads out to find out.When Bai Xiangning came out of the kitchen with the rice dumpling leaves, she saw the people outside stretching their necks with eager expressions on their faces.The boss is out. Hurry up and stand still. It's about to start.The few people who were standing scattered suddenly straightened up, staring intently at the rice dumpling leaves in Bai Xiangning's hand.Bai Xiangning laughed. Seeing them like this, she thought she was about to perform some stunt.But when people wanted to see it, she had no reason to hide it, so she walked to the counter openly and started wrapping the rice dumplings.Traditional triangular rice dumplings are made by rolling rice dumpling leaves into a funnel shape, adding fillings, folding the corners of the rice dumpling leaves, and finally tying them tightly with cotton thread, and a rice dumpling is wrapped.The dice rice dumplings made by Bai Xiangning are similar to woven bamboo baskets. The rice dumpling leaves are processed into long strips, interspersed and interlaced under Bai Xiangning's slender and flexible fingers, and closed into a cube, with both ends inserted into adjacent gaps. Then fill it with stuffing, cross-seal the top rice dumpling leaves, pull the rice dumpling leaves tighter, and finally cut off the excess rice dumpling leaves, and a delicate dice rice dumpling will appear perfectly in front of everyone.Wow, Mom, this zongzi is so magical. A three or four-year-old girl was lying in her mother's arms, her eyes widened, her mouth opened in an O shape, and she said with surprise.She tugged on her mother's sleeves and said coquettishly: "Mom, can you make rice dumplings like this for me when you go back"Her mother was shocked and quickly covered her little chubby girl's mouth. The rice dumplings were so complicated to wrap, but she actually wanted to let her go home to make them.This fucking kidIf she wanted, she could just buy a few more. Is there anything money can't solveSo the mother covered her daughter's mouth with one hand and said with a smile: Boss, I want the remaining rice dumplings. Please help me pack them. Thank you.There were only three or four wrapped rice dumplings left on the counter. Bai Xiangning put them all into a plastic bag. After handing the bag to the mother, the little girl in her arms kept staring at the rice dumpling she had just wrapped. There was a trace of desire in his eyes.Now, this is for you. Bai Xiangning smiled at the little girl, and then handed the rice dumplings made on the spot to the little girl.The little girl stretched out her chubby little hands and carefully took the rice dumplings.This rice dumpling is not big, but when placed in the little girl's hand, it occupies the entire palm of her hand, like a Rubik's cube, lying there quietly.This rice dumpling is so beautiful, like the color of grass. The little girl touched the rice dumplings and said in a serious tone.The appearance of the uncooked rice dumplings is green and green, with interlaced colors, fresh and full of vitality. Unlike the cooked rice dumplings, the leaves have turned brown and are not eye-catching at all.After watching the live performance of making rice dumplings, everyone had a new understanding of Bai Xiangning's dexterity. The rice dumplings looked very complicated, but in Bai Xiangning's hands, they turned out to be a very simple thing. It seemed that with just a few flips of his fingers, a dice dumpling took shape.Just now, her process of making rice dumplings was filmed by one person.After everyone dispersed, Su Yutong walked to Bai Xiangning, "Boss Bai, look at how I took the photo. Have you fully demonstrated your superb skills"Bai Xiangning patiently watched the entire video. I have to say that Su Yutong did a good job with the close-up when it was time to take a close-up, and the long shot when it was time to take a long shot. In her hands, a simple rice dumpling seemed to have turned into a Documentary.You took such a good shot. Bai Xiangning admired her very much.Right, right I feel the same way. Su Yutong is very proud. She usually likes to shoot daily videos. Over time, her shooting skills have become better and better.Su Yutong thought of something and said: By the way, Boss Bai, why don't you create a video account to promote your storeBefore Xiao Qian came here, she didn't even search for Bai's Little Restaurant on the Internet, and said it was a little-known store. Su Yutong felt aggrieved for the little restaurant when she thought about it. It was obviously such a good restaurant, but it lacked publicity. .These days, no matter how good a store is, it would be useless without publicity.Video numberBai Xiangning rarely surfs the Internet and knows basically nothing about short video websites, so when Su Yutong mentioned it, she was still a little confused.Su Yutong clicked on the software she often used and introduced them to Bai Xiangning one by one.This is Xiaocheng Book, where many people share their daily life, including food, travel, movies and other content.This is DouLe. There are many different types of videos on it. Su Yutong randomly clicked on the homepage of a food blogger. Boss Bai, look, this blogger is also a food blogger and now has hundreds of thousands of fans.Boss Bai, the dishes you cook are so beautiful and creative. If you make a video and post it on the Internet, it will definitely get more people's attention.Su Yutong had added Bai Xiangning's WeChat account before. She said excitedly, "Boss Bai, I'll send you the video I just took."Bai Xiangning's cell phone dinged, and the video was quickly received. She looked at Su Yutong, not quite understanding what she meant.Su Yutong was a little embarrassed. She tugged at the end of her hair, and then lowered her voice, "Boss Bai, didn't you just say that my photography was pretty good I just wanted to send you this video. If you don't mind it, You can send it to the video accountIs that okay But this is what you took. It wouldn't be good for me to use it directly.What's wrong with this I just took it casually. If Boss Bai is willing to use this as the first video of your video account, I'll be happy before it's too late.Bai Xiangning thought for a moment, and then said: OK.She added, can you wait for me here for a whilesureSu Yutong thought Bai Xiangning was going to register a video account, and asked her to wait here so that she could ask her if she didn't understand something.Anyway, she and Xiao Qian didn't have any other plans for the evening, so it wouldn't hurt to sit here and wait.The two of them watched the new drama together for a while. After watching the beginning, Bai Xiangning came over.She handed the things she was carrying to Su Yutong and Xiao Qian. I think you like eating rice dumplings, so I just went to the kitchen to wrap some more and give them to you.Bai Xiangning smiled at them as a thank you gift for taking the video.Ah, is this for usSu Yutong and Xiao Qian were flattered. They didn't expect that Boss Bai just went to make rice dumplings for them. The bag was full. Boss Bai was too thoughtful.

Chapter 18Bai Xiangning's previously established customer base now has more than a thousand people. She would read the messages in it at first, but then she gave up when she realized that she couldn't read them all. She only occasionally Open it and take a look.She clicked on the group message, and unsurprisingly it showed 99+.She originally wanted to send a message directly there, but with the speed at which the group members refreshed their screens, her message would soon be lost in the tide.So she posted a group announcement: Everyone can follow the video account of the small restaurant.A link is attached at the bottom of the announcement.After Su Yutong told her about the video account, she downloaded all the well-known video software, then chose the most suitable one to register an account, and then sent the homepage link to the group.This was the first time Bai Xiangning made a group announcement after establishing the group, and the members inside immediately became excited.What This is the video account of a small restaurant. It's here. I must be the first fan.late. I'm the first one hahaha This person posted a screenshot, which is the homepage of the small restaurant, with 1 follower count.Ah ah ah, damn it, you are trying to steal my number one spot. The person who just clamored to be the first fan comforted himself, it doesn't matter, it doesn't matter, if you can't be number one, you can be among the first hundred.But he has never used the software that Bai Xiangning is using before, and now he has to download and register it. When he completes the process, he will follow Bai Xiangning's video account.He looked at the message that popped up on the screen: Congratulations on becoming the 101st fan of Bai Family Restaurant, and fell into a long silence.Before Bai Xiangning's group announcement, she had already posted her first video on her homepage, which was the one Su Yutong sent her.The play count quickly exceeded 100, and every time it was refreshed, there would be many more comments below.Wow wow wow, Boss Bai is so skillful.It's so magical. It turns out that this rice dumpling is made like this. Okay, my eyes are used to it. I'll try it tomorrow.My eyes told me that I knew it, but my hands stopped me. I admire Boss Bai so much that he can make tricks out of ordinary rice dumplings.Woohoo, I'm so greedy again. I'm going to buy a few more tomorrow to soothe my wounded heart.Boss Bai, please make sure to post more videos like this in the future. I love watching them.Love to watch +1Boss Bai, please feel free to post videos. I will come to support you in every video you make from now on.Seeing everyone's enthusiastic comments, Bai Xiangning couldn't help but smile.Soon, there was another group announcement in the group.Thank you very much for your support. Every time a new dish is released in the future, it will be sent to the video account simultaneously.Although the first video posted was of her making rice dumplings, Bai Xiangning has considered that subsequent videos will focus more on the display of finished products. Videos are more concrete than text, allowing customers to see the dishes intuitively, and are more likely to attract customers. Reach new customers to taste it, thereby achieving the purpose of expanding your popularity.The two days in Jinghua City passed quickly, and Xiao Qian got on the high-speed train for the return trip. She had the rice dumplings that Bai Xiangning had given her before.Su Yutong sent her on the high-speed rail, and before leaving, she gave her share to Xiao Qian.Xiao Qian still wanted to refuse, but Su Yutong stopped her with one sentence, "Just keep it. You won't be able to eat in the restaurant anyway when you go back. I live here, and I can eat whenever I want."Xiao Qian:Okay, then she accepts it. It would be rude to be polite.Xiao Qian got into the car with a smile on her face and her heart was pounding.Just like Su Yutong said, she won't be able to eat in a small restaurant after taking this train.I really want to cancel my ticket and stay in Jinghua City, but I have to go to work tomorrow and the social worker has no choice.The car started slowly, Xiao Qian held the window open and watched Su Yutong's figure getting further and further away.She knew that after leaving this station, Su Yutong would go straight to the small restaurant and have a hearty meal.Not her share.Fortunately, she still had a big bag of fresh rice dumplings. She took them back and put them in the refrigerator to eat later.I don't know if my mother will make rice dumplings this year.Xiao Qian made a video call to her mother, who was quickly connected. As soon as her mother saw her precious daughter, the smile on her face immediately expanded several times.Qianqian was wearing an apron and seemed to be busy with something.Xiao Qian couldn't help but send a big smile to her mother, "Mom, what are you doing"Her mother immediately raised what she was holding and was making rice dumplings.Xiao Qian moved closer to the screen, trying to see what kind of rice dumplings her mother was making. Her mother raised the half-wrapped rice dumplings closer to the screen so that her daughter could see them more clearly.It's candied date rice dumplings that she loves the mostHmm, it's your favorite candied date rice dumplings. I'll send you some after mom wraps them up.A warm current surged through Xiao Qian's heart.To be honest, my mother's skills in making rice dumplings have never been very good, but because she likes to eat them, she makes them every year.Sometimes the rice dumplings were not tightly wrapped, and some of the glutinous rice inside would be exposed when cooked, but she would eat them all every time without wasting any.She looked at the rice dumplings in the bag at hand. The rice dumplings were exquisite in shape and skillful, and much prettier than those made by her mother.However, she recalled the taste in her memory.The rice dumplings made by my mother taste as good as anyone else's.It's the taste of home.It is an irreplaceable and incomparable taste.She suddenly wanted to go back.This year during the Dragon Boat Festival, she had to fight with the company to take two more days off, and then go home to give her parents a big surprise.Xiao Qian secretly made up her mind.

Chapter 19On Saturday, Wang Yalei got up early and rushed to the high-speed rail station.His parents came by car from the next city today, and he went to pick them up.Wang Yalei waited at the exit for a while, and then saw his parents walking out carrying large and small bags.Parents hereHe hadn't seen his parents for a long time. Wang Yalei waved to them excitedly. After they left the station, he immediately grabbed their luggage. "Mom and dad, give it to me to carry."He carried the bag, and then took the bag from his mother's hand.When you weigh it, it's quite heavy.Mom, what's in hereAfter her son took the things over, Xie Rong felt a lot more relaxed. Looking at her son who had grown to 1.8 meters, she felt very pleased that her son was sensible.She wiped the sweat from her forehead and said: This is a hometown specialty brought for you. Didn't you still want to eat it two days agoWang Yalei felt the weight in his hand. The contents of this bag were estimated to be four to five kilograms.His parents came all the way to see him and still didn't forget to bring him so many things. Seeing the sweat on his parents' foreheads, Wang Yalei felt sour and moved.He had booked a hotel near the school in advance, a slightly more expensive one, just to make his parents' stay more comfortable.It just so happened that he would also do part-time jobs on weekends and save some money.After settling their parents, they blew on the air conditioner in the hotel for a while.After the heat faded, the hunger caused by the fatigue of traveling and traveling also came back.Wang Yalei's father, Wang Hai, asked his son: Didn't you say last time that you would take us to eat in that small restaurantIt's Bai's small restaurant. Wang Yalei added, I told my boss in advance yesterday that I can just go directly later.Bai's little restaurantIt doesn't sound like a very famous store.But after all, it was his son who chose it, so Wang Hai and Xie Rong didn't say anything. This time when they came to Jinghua City, their son had already greeted them in advance, saying that he would be responsible for all expenses and that they did not need to worry.They were deeply relieved and felt that their son suddenly became much more reliable. If the son has this intention, the parents must also consider the child's financial situation. The son is not officially working yet, so he only works part-time on weekends, and he certainly does not have much savings.If you take them to eat in a fancy restaurant, it will put a burden on the children, which is not their intention.Wang Yalei took his parents to the snack street. There were various stores on the street selling everything.But we were almost at the end, and my son didn't stop. Instead, he was still walking forward.Seeing that Xie Rong was about to reach the end of the street, she asked: Son, which store are you going to take us to Aren't there so many stores where we passed beforeWang Yalei pointed to the front and said: Just walk to the corner over there and you'll be there.Which store would open in such a remote place The front of this street is so busy, the customers must have gathered there. Who can be around this cornerXie Rong then thought about it, maybe her son didn't want them to wait any longer, so he deliberately chose a store with fewer people.After arriving at Bai's small restaurant, they realized that what they had just thought was terribly wrong.Who said there are few people hereThese people are almost queuing up to the door of the store.Wang Hai was surprised and said: Why are there so many peopleThe location of this store is not good, but it can still attract so many customersThere are always a lot of people in the small restaurant. Wang Yalei scratched his head, Mom and Dad, let's go in first. Boss Bai has left a small box for us.Seeing Wang Yalei, Qiao Ping warmly greeted them to the box on the second floor.I don't know if it was Wang Hai's illusion, but from the moment they went up to the second floor, many people's eyes followed them until they entered the box.Those eyes were full of envy, jealousy and hatred.It made his back feel cold.Bai Xiangning put a lot of thought into the decoration of the box. The styles of the two boxes are different. The one Wang Yalei and the others are in is a small box with light-colored wooden floors. The light from the chandelier is soft and not dazzling. The walls are decorated with stickers. With the warm-colored wallpaper, the entire box looks very warm, which is very suitable for a family or a group of friends to gather for dinner.The environment inside is also very clean and looks very comfortable.After they sat down, Qiao Ping quickly came in with a dish.The fragrance immediately filled the entire box.What does this smell like It smells sour and so fragrant. Xie Rong felt like her stomach was protesting under the temptation of the aroma.Qiao Ping placed the first dish on the table. This dish was served in a casserole. After opening the lid, the aroma that had been subtle just now poured out without hesitation.Good, it smells good, Wang Hai murmured.What came up was a dish of beef brisket with tomatoes and potatoes. This dish is sweet and sour and tastes appetizing, so I put it first.The addition of tomatoes makes the soup of this dish red and attractive, and even the air is slightly sweet and sour, stimulating people's appetite.Dad, Mom, eat quickly.Seeing his parents' reactions, Wang Yalei knew that they were shocked by the fragrance.Wang Yalei had the same reaction when he ate it for the first time, but now that he is a regular customer of the restaurant, his tolerance is much higher than before, so he can still stay calm when he smells such a fragrance.Of course, it only lasts ten seconds.No one can survive the delicious onslaught of a bistro for ten seconds, no one.Tomato, potato and beef brisket is a dish with a lot of soup. Wang Yalei used a spoon to serve it into a small bowl for his parents to make it easier for them to eat.Xie Nan picked up a piece of beef brisket and took a bite. The juice was rich in sweetness and sourness. As his teeth clenched, it filled his mouth, and his sleeping taste buds were instantly awakened. The first thing you feel when you enter your mouth is the sour and sweet taste of tomatoes wrapped on the surface of beef. After chewing, the rich milky flavor unique to beef brisket comes out, making your mouth water.Xie Rong picked up the second piece almost immediately.This beef brisket is so deliciousThe beef brisket has meat and tendons, alternating between fat and lean, and is extremely soft when stewed. The most difficult-to-cook beef tendons have become soft and trembling between the two chopsticks.

When you bite into it, it is soft, glutinous, delicious, and extremely mellow.She poured the soup and meat on the rice, and the bright red soup seeped into the rice instantly. She mixed it and swallowed it in one gulp, feeling great satisfaction in her stomach.The tomatoes were peeled and simmered for a long time, and all the juice inside melted into the dish and merged with the beef brisket. The potatoes are also stewed just right, almost melting in your mouth, dense and smooth.This dish was so filling that before the next dish was served, Xie Rong and Wang Hai had already eaten a large bowl of rice.Wang Yalei did not hesitate to give in and ate a bowl and a half.Xie Rong put down her chopsticks and praised: "The taste of this restaurant is really good." She looked at Wang Yalei, "Son, the level of restaurants in Jinghua City is very high, right Even such an inconspicuous restaurant on the roadside tastes so good, what about other big hotels" How delicious the food isWang Yalei shook his head, Mom, you guessed wrong.Xie Rong was puzzled.Wang Yalei continued: To be honest, this restaurant is the best one among the many restaurants I have eaten at in Jinghua City.

Chapter 20If she had heard her son speak so highly of a roadside shop before coming here, Xie Rong would have felt that he was exaggerating.But now that she has almost finished the beef brisket in the casserole, she naturally agrees with her son's views.The location of this store is not very good, but whether it is the decoration of the store or the quality of the dishes, it is not difficult to see the owner's intentions.Only with enough attentiveness can you attract so many guests despite insufficient congenital conditions.Although he had already eaten a lot, Xie Rong's chopsticks still involuntarily reached for the last piece of beef brisket in the casserole.By coincidence, Wang Hai and Wang Yalei's chopsticks also reached for the piece of beef brisket at the same time.When the tops of the three pairs of chopsticks touched, the air suddenly became silent.Xie Rong took the initiative and stared at Wang Hai, "Husband, don't you usually like beef Let me take care of this for you."Wang Hai's chopsticks showed no tendency to retreat at all. He said calmly: It's okay to eat occasionally. Wife, you've eaten so much beef, it's time to take a rest.Wang Yalei tried to snatch the last piece of beef brisket while his parents were bickering.But before he could make any move, Xie Rong and Wang Hai both looked at him. Wang Yalei shivered at the sight and silently retracted his hand that wanted to pinch the meat.He comforted himself in his heart, it didn't matter, he was in Jinghua City anyway, and there would be many opportunities to eat at small restaurants in the future, so it would be better for his parents to eat more.In the end, the piece of beef brisket fell into Xie Rong's bowl. She calmly put the beef brisket into her mouth under the envious eyes of the father and son, and swallowed it with satisfaction.The rich beef juice mixed with the rich tomato and potato soup entered her stomach, and she was still a little unsatisfied after finishing the meal.Wang Hai looked at the casserole with only a little soup left in it, his eyes full of resentment.But they didn't have to wait long as the second dish was brought out.This dish is placed in a bamboo steamer. After it is served to the table, the heat inside rises through the steamer, raising the surrounding temperature.What kind of dish is thisQiao Ping opened the lid of the steamer. This was steamed pork.The moment the lid was opened, all three people on the table took a deep breath in unison.I can't wait to inhale all this rich fragrance into my stomach.The brown steamed pork powder tightly wraps the pork belly, and the fat of the pork belly penetrates into the rice noodles after steaming, adding a few oily colors to the rice noodles. The steamed pork noodles are stacked together in the steamer, tempting people. taste.This time Wang Hai reacted the fastest and immediately picked up a piece of steamed pork and bit it.The first thing you feel on the tip of your tongue is the grainy texture of steamed pork rice noodles, and then comes the pork belly that melts in your mouth. The oil has been steamed and is crystal clear, leaving a mouthful of fragrance after one bite.Bai Xiangning did not buy ready-made steamed pork powder outside, but chose to make it herself. First put the rice and Sichuan pepper aniseed ingredients into a pot and stir-fry continuously. When the rice turns yellow and swells, pour it out and beat it into powder with a blender. You don't need to beat it too finely to keep the graininess of the aniseed ingredients. To bring a unique aroma different from rice to the taste buds.Xie Rong actually didn't like eating pork belly very much, but seeing how delicious Wang Hai ate it, she couldn't help but taste a piece.As soon as the tip of her tongue touched the steamed pork, Xie Rong's eyes were filled with surprise.The pork belly has been steamed at high temperature and is so tender that it melts in your mouth without chewing. It is fresh and plump but not greasy at all.This must be made from the best black soil pork. Xie Rong has been in charge of the kitchen all year round and is very familiar with the ingredients, so she ate it as soon as she ate it.She was right, Bai Xiangning used local pork. That pork shop is the only one in the market that sells local pork. The price is several yuan more expensive than other shops, but the business is still very good. His shop has the most people queuing up every time. If I had gone a little later, there wouldn't even be any scraps of meat left.Bai Xiangning went there early specially to buy such a beautiful piece of Wuhua.After his parents had eaten several pieces, Wang Yalei started to taste it. This time, his parents came all the way here. They should have been given good food and drink, but he couldn't compete with them.Wang Yalei's movements were a little harder, but he didn't expect that the piece of meat was directly clamped in half. Wang Yalei picked up one half, and the fat part at the break had become crystal clear, while the thin part had become crystal clear. The meat is a light brownish-pink color, with layers of lean meat and fat meat overlapping each other, making it look mouth-watering.Take a bite and the full meat juice will overflow, leaving you with endless aftertaste.The pork belly that Boss Bai chose was really good. It was neither too fat nor too thin, and it tasted just right. Wang Yalei praised while eating.Xie Rong picked up a piece of steamed pork and put it into a bowl. She used chopsticks to remove the rice noodles wrapped on it. The pork belly inside was exposed. The ratio of fat to thin was perfectly distributed, almost 50-50. So only after steaming can it have the right taste.Wang Hai couldn't stop eating. He loved this steamed pork so much.The proportion of fat in the meat is just right, so the whole dish will not be full of fat after steaming. The excess fat that seeps out is absorbed by the steamed pork powder outside, making it look shiny and light in the mouth. , not greasy or heavy at all.The airtightness of the steamer is very good, and the steamed meat powder wraps the meat extremely tightly. Under this double guarantee, the flavor of the meat will not leak out at all. Only at the moment when the teeth touch, the rich meat juice locked inside will pour out and firmly occupy every corner of the mouth.The mouthful is full of mellow meaty aroma, and you can't taste the greasiness of fatty meat at all. The amount of spices in the steamed pork powder is not too much or too little, so after adding it, it does not overwhelm the others.

Instead, it makes the meaty aroma of the pork belly more intense.This dish is very homely, but the more homely it is, the harder it is to make it delicious.Whether it's steamed pork rice noodles or pork belly, no matter which ingredient is not up to standard, the finished dish cannot be presented so perfectly.Wang Hai couldn't help but sigh, this restaurant must have hired a chef who has been in the industry for decades. The taste is really unique.Wang Yalei knew that Bai Xiangning was both the boss and the chef. He recalled Bai Xiangning's appearance and found that she didn't look like someone who had been working in the industry for decades.Dad, Mom, as far as I know, the chef in this store is only in his early twenties.Wang Hai was so shocked that he even dropped the meat between his chopsticks. He quickly picked it up and put it in his mouth. After swallowing it completely, he hurriedly asked, "There are only two chefs in this restaurant." teenagersWang Yalei nodded, yes, when we walked in just now, the person standing at the counter was the chef. He is also the boss.Wang Hai and Xie Rong were stunned at the same time. They were impressed by Bai Xiangning. When they entered the door, they secretly sighed that this girl's appearance was too outstanding.Unexpectedly, he became a restaurant owner at such a young age. What's even more amazing is her superb cooking skills. The dishes she cooks are not inferior to those of some long-established restaurants.Xie Rong sighed: The boss is really awesome, he is so young and his craftsmanship is so good.Wang Yalei was convinced.The boss is not only good at his craftsmanship, he is also very kind and patient with every customer, making them feel like spring breeze.Soon, the basket of steamed rice noodles was almost eaten, revealing the vegetables underneath.Hey, this is taroXie Rong picked up a piece and after eating it, she realized it was taro.The taro absorbs the oily aroma of the pork belly, and tastes mellow, soft, and smooth. It melts on the tip of the tongue with a slight sip.This taro is also delicious. Try it now.Originally, Wang Hai and Wang Yalei both put down their chopsticks, but after hearing what Xie Rong said, they couldn't help but move their chopsticks.Delicious. Wang Yalei accidentally ate the whole piece of taro. I have never eaten such delicious taro.The three of them didn't even miss the taro, and each of them picked up a few pieces. At this time, the entire steamed pork dish was really at its bottom, and only the lotus leaves were left in the steamer.The sound of footsteps came from the stairwell, and Qiao Ping quickly knocked on the door and came in.This time she served several dishes. Wang Yalei took a look and found that they were all dishes he had eaten before.There are three cups of chicken, plum pork ribs, and mapo tofu.Qiao Ping finished serving the food and was about to go down. Wang Hai called out to her and asked, "Can you help me serve more rice"The three of them had already finished the rice they had served before, leaving only a few grains of rice stained on the inner wall of the plate.Qiao Ping responded: Okay, wait a moment, I will serve you some rice.Please give me more trouble. Wang Yalei added.She smiled and said: Yes, I know, you have to eat three big bowls of rice every time you come here. I'll get more. I'll make sure you're full.He often comes here to eat. Qiao Ping is familiar with him and knows that this young man has a big appetite. After she finished speaking, she trotted downstairs. There were many guests today, so her movements were more agile than usual.As soon as Qiao Ping came downstairs, Xie Rong and Wang Hai both looked at their son.Wang Yalei felt embarrassed when they looked at him, and felt a little guilty for no reason. After all, they had said before that the restaurants outside were unhygienic and told him to eat less outside.As Qiao Ping said just now, her parents must know that he often comes here to eat, and they don't know if they will talk about him.Wang Yalei was worried for a moment, and then Xie Rong spoke.I did tell him, but the content was different from what he expected.Xie Ronggang's first reaction when she learned that her son often eats here is, "Why did you bring us here because there is such a delicious restaurant"Wang Yalei said nonchalantly: "Isn't this your first time coming to Jinghua City I brought you here to eat as soon as you arrived."Xie Rong hates the fact that iron cannot be transformed into steel. If you had told us that there was such a delicious restaurant here, your dad and I would have come here a long time agoahDad, Mom, you don't look like the kind of people who would come here just for a meal.Wang Yalei couldn't help but feel sad, feeling that he was not as good as a meal in the hearts of his parents.But then he thought about it and felt that if it were him, he would come here to eat.Because the small restaurant is really worth itWang Hai tasted all three new dishes. Every dish was so delicious that he wanted to swallow it with his tongue.He said to Wang Yalei: Son, you are studying in college away from home, and your mother and I are thinking about you. Otherwise, we will come to see you once a month in the future.Xie Rong also stood on her husband's side. She nodded: Yes, even though you are such an adult, you still don't take good care of yourself. You can rest assured that your parents often come to see you. a little.Wang Yalei:You'd better really come and see me.Wang Yalei said deliberately: Okay, next time you come over, I will take you to eat the most famous Wei Dingji in Jinghua City.Wei Ding Ji is a time-honored brand in Jinghua City, with chain stores all over the city. A few years ago, Wang Yalei's parents went to eat there and were amazed by the taste for a long time.Before coming this time, they thought their son would take them to eat there, but now after trying Bai's Little Restaurant, they didn't miss Wei Dingji at all.There is no need to take us to eat at Wei Ding Ji. I think this small restaurant is good. The dishes are full of flavor and color, and the prices are affordable. It is especially suitable for our family of three to eat. Xie Rong closed her eyes and started to praise the small restaurant. She wanted me to Let me tell you, although Wei Dingji is very famous, its reputation is very fictitious, and it is still a real small restaurant.While they were talking, Wang Hai put the last piece of three-cup chicken in the casserole into his bowl, and then said calmly: I think your mother is right. Although Wei Ding Ji is a large chain restaurant, in terms of taste alone, it is still better than the small restaurants.Wang Yalei's eyes lit up, "Yeah, right" The first time I ate at a small restaurant, I thought it was better than Wei Dingji, but I didn't dare to say it at the time, for fear of being criticized by others.He was about to eat another piece of three-cup chicken, but when he saw the empty casserole and the piece of chicken in his father's bowl, he wanted to cry without tears.Wow, so cruel.He used to think that his parents didn't pay much attention to verbal desires.But what can he do He can only let his parents eat it.Just now while they were eating, Qiao Ping served another dish of stir-fried vegetables. As soon as it was brought to the table, the three of them ate half of it.Most of the previous dishes were meat dishes, which would inevitably make them a bit greasy after eating too much. This dish uses seasonal chicken greens, with tender leaves. As soon as you eat it, all the remaining greasy food will be left in your mouth. It absorbs and feels extremely refreshing.Stir-fried vegetables should be regarded as the most common dish. Almost every household can make it. The varieties of vegetables change with the seasons. Generally, the fresh vegetables in season are used.What kind of flowers can be made from such a simple dishBefore Wang Hai ate it, he thought it was similar to what was fried at home, but when he actually ate it, he was still amazed.Oh my gosh, this dish is so crispy and tender.When you bite into it, you can even clearly hear the crisp sound of the vegetable leaves being bitten off, and the sound of juice splashing out.Xie Rong was also very surprised.Stir-fried vegetables is a dish that is served almost every day at her house. She doesn't know how many times she has made it, but every time the vegetables she stir-fries are wilted. Yes, it doesn't taste crispy at all.But the stir-fried chicken vegetables cooked in the small restaurant were completely different from what she had eaten before.The surface of the vegetable leaves is covered with a thin layer of oil. The leaves look shiny, green and plump. The moisture inside is firmly locked and not lost at all, so it tastes very crisp and not dry at all. .The three of them each had chopsticks, and they devoured a plate full of stir-fried chicken and vegetables in no time.At this time, Qiao Ping brought up the last dish.This isWang Yalei sat up a little straighter and looked closer. The dishes that had just been served were colorful and eye-catching.There were corn kernels, peas, carrots, and that little one inside. Wang Yalei didn't recognize what it was for a while.These are pine nuts. Xie Rong said.Qiao Ping smiled and introduced: This last dish is called Jin Yu Man Tang, which means happiness and happiness. It was specially made by Boss Bai.Xie Rong said in surprise: Oh, the boss is so thoughtful.Wang Yalei continued to be a filial and good boy. He picked up the white porcelain spoon placed next to the plate and scooped some for his parents.The taste of this last dish is light, without too much seasoning, and it tastes very refreshing.The corn is golden, each grain is plump, and the taste is sweet. The pine nuts are fried and have a crispy outer skin. When eaten, there will be a unique aroma of nuts in your mouth.The combination of these ingredients not only makes them look beautiful in color, but also blends the flavors very harmoniously, making it full of color, flavor and aroma.They almost ate this dish as an after-dinner snack. After eating, Wang Yalei and his parents leaned on the backs of their chairs, touched their belly that was about to burst, and said with satisfaction: Phew, you're full. If there wasn't really any room in my stomach, I could keep eating. Wang Yalei always has a big appetite. Even he said he was full today, but you can only imagine how much he ate.Xie Rong doesn't like to eat much at night, but she broke the habit today and ate two bowls of rice. Now she clearly felt that the skirt on her body was a little tight.Wang Hai was carefree and didn't care about his image. He didn't care that his belly was stretching out his shirt.It's rare to come across such a delicious restaurant, isn't it normal to eat moreBecause they were so full after eating, it was very difficult to stand up, so the three of them sat and digested for a while. When their stomachs were no longer so full, they stood up and prepared to go downstairs.Finished eatingAs soon as she came down the stairs, she met Bai Xiangning who was walking towards the hall. When she saw them coming down, Bai Xiangning stopped and said hello to them.I didn't look carefully when I came in before, but now I'm closer. Xie Rong took a look and thought that the owner of this shop is really handsome. Not only is he handsome, but he also cooks well. He is really young and promising.She took a step forward and said to Bai Xiangning: Boss Bai, thank you for your hospitality. The dishes on the table just now are enough for me to remember for a month. I heard my son say that you are not only the owner of this shop, but also the chef. Is it rightBai Xiangning nodded.Xie Rong looked at her with a hint of admiration in her eyes. Boss Bai, the food you cook is so delicious. With such good skills at such a young age, your store will definitely get better and better.She spoke sincerely, and her tone of voice showed her trust in Bai Xiangning. She seemed to have no doubt that she would develop the small restaurant even better in the future.Anyone who hears such praise for himself will be very helpful, and Bai Xiangning is no exception.She smiled and said to Xie Rong: Your satisfaction with the food is the greatest affirmation for me.The next day, Wang Yalei took his parents to visit the famous scenic spots in Jinghua City. It was a rare visit for them and they must have a great time.The three of them played from morning till dusk, visiting all the botanical gardens, zoos, and aquariums in Jinghua City. In the end, they were so tired that they couldn't even lift their legs.Xie Rong was the first to surrender. No, I can't anymore. I can't walk a step anymore. We have been playing for so long and have been to all the places we should go. It's time to take a rest.Wang Hai's back was covered in sweat. The weather was very hot now and there were many people at the attractions. They spent most of the day queuing and kept walking after entering. Not to mention how tired they were. .He fanned the wind with his hands and panted and said: Son, let's go to the small restaurant yesterday for dinner quickly, and then your mother and I are going to go back by car.Yes, my stomach is almost starving. Now I just want to go to a small restaurant and I don't want to go anywhere.All right. Wang Yalei originally wanted to take them to the mall to buy something, but now it seems that it is best for his parents to go straight to the small restaurant.They didn't take the bus, but took a taxi directly.The air conditioner in the taxi was turned on very much, and they felt much cooler. Xie Rong thought of something and said to Wang Yalei: By the way, son, hurry up and book a box with Boss Bai, just the one we went to yesterday.Xie Rong thought that the private room in the small restaurant could be reserved on the day, but Wang Yalei felt bitter when he heard it.Mom, do you know how difficult it is to book a private room in a small restaurantBut didn't you make the reservation yesterdayHey, it's a long storyWang Hai interrupted his son, then you can make the story short. Your mother and I are in a hurry to eat.So Wang Yalei told his parents in detail how he got the box yesterday.After he finished speaking, he said pitifully: Now you know, rightWang Hai and Xie Rong did not answer, but lowered their heads and pressed the screen of their mobile phones.Wang Yalei took a closer look and found that there was an orange-yellow software with the icon of a big pot on both of their mobile phones.It's the one he developed for the small restaurant.Looking again, my parents actually registered their accounts. After registering, they clicked into the box reservation interface, and sure enough they found that today's box had been booked.Dad and Mom Wang Yalei thought that his parents would be very disappointed, but Xie Rong suddenly raised his head and said to him,Son, you are really proud of your parents.Ah, Wang Yalei hasn't reacted yet.Xie Rong smiled, you made this software, right I didn't expect that our son is now so powerful, and the software he developed is used by so many people.If no one uses it, the private rooms for a month will not be fully booked.Wang Yalei felt embarrassed after hearing his mother's words.He said modestly: Actually, I didn't do anything. The restaurant had too many loyal customers, so I just took advantage of it.Wang Hai patted his shoulder. Think about it, if the software you made was not good, Boss Bai would have asked Boss Bai to change the software. How could he continue to use yoursWhen Wang Yalei thought about it, it seemed to be the truth.Wang Hai continued: I just took a look at the software you made. It runs without any lag at all. The interface is also simple and well done.He is not a professional, he just evaluates Wang Yalei's software from the perspective of customer use.Wang Hai really thinks that his son's software is great.With the encouragement of his parents, Wang Yalei also began to feel great.Not to mention other things, just saying that the small restaurant's exclusive software is made by him is enough to make people proud, okayButbut there is no box todayWhen he thought of this, Wang Yalei's mood became depressed again. He wanted his parents to spend this day without regrets.When Xie Rong saw her son's expression, she knew what he was thinking. She said in a relaxed tone: Oh, why are you so frustrated There is no private room, so the three of us can sit outside. Okay, isn't there even a table for three people outsideYes, I have.That's alright, let's sit outside. It's more lively outside.After they arrived at the store, they had to wait for a while to find seats, but their parents didn't seem to mind at all, so Wang Yalei no longer bothered about the lack of private rooms.As soon as he entered the door, Wang Yalei noticed that there was a large bucket at the door, with a note on it, iced mung bean soup, 2 yuan a bowl.Wang Yalei lightly touched the surface of the big iron bucket, and his fingers were immediately frozen. Just standing next to the big bucket, he could feel the chill.Wouldn't it be more enjoyable if you had a bowl like thatBoss, please serve three bowls of mung bean soup first. Wang Yalei said to Bai Xiangning.Qiao Ping served each of them a bowl of mung bean soup. After a few mouthfuls, the restlessness and heat that had been scorched by the sun for a day immediately subsided a lot.Wang Hai put down the empty bowl and said: After drinking this bowl, I feel much more comfortable, and I don't feel so hot.Xie Rong also smiled and said: "My appetite has recovered a lot."They also ordered a lot of dishes tonight, and every dish, without exception, was on a disc.After eating, Wang Yalei and his parents returned to the hotel. After taking their luggage, they set off to the station to prepare to take the train back.Wang Yalei walked them into the ticket gate and waited until they checked in before leaving.After getting on the train, Xie Rong happily said to her husband: Our son is becoming more and more mature now. We don't have to worry about anything these two days. He can arrange everything after him. All right.Yes, my son has really grown up and is reliable.The two were silent for a moment, and suddenly they said in unison: The restaurant is really delicious.They looked at each other and smiled, and Xie Rong continued: When we come back next time, the small restaurant will definitely serve new dishes. Then let my son book a private room in advance, and we can have a hearty meal.

Chapter 21Uncle Chen was lying on the recliner, holding a newspaper in his left hand and fanning slowly with his right hand. He felt very comfortable.When the weather got hot, people were too lazy to move. Mrs. Chen didn't want to be busy in the kitchen at noon, so she said to Uncle Chen: Old man, let's just order some noodles for lunch.Uncle Chen pulled his wife onto the recliner and stood up by himself. Stop working. It's such a hot day and you don't have the appetite to eat.He walked to the kitchen, took a look, and then said: There was some cold noodles left from last night, so I can eat some for lunch.After I finished speaking, I didn't wait for a response. When I looked back, I saw that my wife was leaning on the recliner and taking a nap. Uncle Chen laughed and took a thin blanket to cover his wife. Although it was hot now, their old bones were not as good as those of young people and they could easily catch cold.Grandpa ChenSuddenly a familiar voice came from outside. Uncle Chen walked out and saw Bai Xiangning walking towards here carrying a lunch box.Grandpa Chen, I made some mung bean soup this morning and brought it over for you and Grandma Chen to try. She placed the lunch box on the table at Uncle Chen's house and opened the lid.Ouch, you kid, it's so hot outside, why did you come all the way hereIt's not a two-step process and it's not hot. Bai Xiangning smiled carelessly. Despite this, there was actually a little sweat on her forehead.Grandma Chen woke up when she heard the movement. When she saw Bai Xiangning, she immediately smiled and pulled her to a chair to sit down.You're here, sit down and have a rest.I'm not tired. Please try the mung bean soup I made. I cooled some and brought it over.Bai Xiangning went to the kitchen and took two small bowls, and filled a bowl of mung bean soup for Uncle Chen and Grandma Chen. She made it in the morning. Now the heat has basically dissipated and it has become normal temperature.Bai Xiangning previously sold iced mung bean soup in the store, but considering the age of Uncle Chen and the others, their stomachs may not be able to tolerate food that is too cold, so she brought mung bean soup at room temperature, which can also have the effect. Relieving summer heat.Uncle Chen picked up the bowl. The mung beans in it had been boiled to the point of being sandy. The soup was clear and green in color, and small mung beans were floating in it. It looked very cool.He took a sip, and the heat all over his body was immediately soothed, so he couldn't help but drink a few more sips. Soon, the bowl of mung bean soup was empty.Seeing that he kept drinking, his wife also picked up the bowl and started drinking.This mung bean soup doesn't feel so hot after a few sips.When the mung bean soup was about to be cooked, Bai Xiangning put a small piece of sugar in it, so you could taste a hint of sweetness, but it was not so sweet that it was cloying, but just right, and it was refreshing to drink it. The spleen and stomach are relaxed and the spirit is refreshed.Seeing that Uncle Chen's bowl was empty, Bai Xiangning poured some more from the lunch box.She packed the mung bean soup in a lunch box. After Uncle Chen and his wife drank two bowls each, there were only a few remaining blooming mung beans left in the lunch box.Uncle Chen wanted to drink more, but Bai Xiangning said: This mung bean soup is cold in nature, so you shouldn't drink too much. Besides, this soup is watery and cannot be eaten as food. Grandpa Chen and Grandma Chen, it's almost lunch time, why don't you go to my place and have lunch togetherAt noon, she and Qiao Ping were the only two people in Bai Xiangning's shop, plus Uncle Chen and his wife, a total of four people were eating. Bai Xiangning fried a few home-cooked dishes and the meal was served quickly.The air conditioning was turned on in the store, and the air conditioning was very strong. As soon as Uncle Chen and the others came in, they were shivering from the cold.Bai Xiangning adjusted the temperature of the air conditioner in time and raised the wind direction to avoid blowing Uncle Chen and Grandma Chen.After sitting at the dinner table, Grandma Chen looked at the decoration of the store, and recalled how the store looked before. She couldn't help but said: Xiang Ning, you have taken good care of this store, everything is in order. If your parents see it, they will definitely be very happy.Mentioning her parents, Bai

Xiangning's mood dropped for a moment. Grandma Chen looked at her expression and secretly blamed herself for saying so many words. Just when she was about to add a few words, Bai Xiangning said: Even if they can't see it. Well, I don't want to let them down either.Bai Xiangning was able to open a small restaurant, and her parents, who had never met before, also helped her a lot, leaving the store and a sum of money for her.Thinking of the envelope she found in the old box, Bai Xiangning felt a warm current in her heart. What was written on the envelope was a dowry for her. She used the money when she was short of money, but later when the small restaurant made a profit, she made up for it and put it back.Although this dowry may not be used, after all, it is the parents' affection for their children, so it is better to put it back in its original place and treasure it.Grandma Chen regretted that she said something she shouldn't have said, so she changed the subject and said: There are many customers in the store recently, Xiang Ning, can you still be busyBai Xiangning smiled and said: Well, I can keep busy. Besides, Qiao Ping is here. She works hard and quickly. With her helping me, I can relax a lot.Hearing Bai Xiangning praise herself, Qiao Ping felt embarrassed and didn't know what to say, so she could only bury her head in the rice.Grandma Chen smiled when she saw this and said: She is a good and down-to-earth child.Seeing that you are running the store so well now, we can feel relieved. Uncle Chen was worried about Bai Xiangning's store losing money at first, but after a period of observation, he found that the business of the small restaurant was so good that he didn't need to worry at all.There used to be Bai Xiangning's department store on this street, but now it has been converted into a small restaurant. Only Uncle Chen's hardware store is left. Other than that, they are all restaurants. Uncle Chen's Hardware Store The store looks out of place among them.Xiang Ning, the decision you made before was so wise. If you continue to keep the department store, it will definitely be difficult to make ends meet. Now that you have opened a small restaurant, the business is much better than before.Unlike our hardware store, no one comes in all day long. If this wasn't our own store, we would definitely not be able to pay the rent. When he thought of this, Uncle Chen's face became gloomy.Bai Xiangning was about to say a few words of comfort, but Grandma Chen said: What are you telling Xiangning to do We are old and won't be able to do it in another two years. If there are many people in the store, you can greet them. Hearing what his wife said, Uncle Chen immediately thought of the difficult days when he was young. At that time, he was running around outside every day to make a living, and sometimes he didn't even have time to eat. Now that he has his own shop, although there is no business, he has something to do and a place to stay, so he should be content.He chuckled and said: The old lady is right, it is better now, leisurely and clean, and you can listen to the radio and read newspapers from time to time. Where can you find such daysNo, Xiaofeng told me that day that we should retire early.Uncle Chen was shocked, why are you retiringHis wife gave him a blank look, why should he help take care of his grandsonWhen he mentioned bringing up his grandson, Uncle Chen couldn't help but smile. He kept saying: Okay, it's great to bring up your grandson. I don't want to see this store anymore, so I'm going to take my grandson there.Bai Xiangning kept smiling as she listened to what Uncle Chen and his wife were talking about, and would participate in their conversations from time to time. The meal was quickly finished.The short stretch of road approaching the vegetable market was full of retail traders selling fruits and vegetables. When Bai Xiangning passed by, she noticed a stall selling lychees.The vendor was arranging the lychees in the basket. When he saw someone stopping in front of him, he raised his head and greeted warmly: "Would you like lychees I just brought them here. They are very fresh and very sweet."Bai Xiangning squatted down, and the vendor broke a lychee from a branch and handed it to her, "Girl, please try it, this lychee is very sweet."She peeled it open and put it in her mouth. The extremely sweet juice immediately made her feel a little cool in this hot summer.This lychee is so sweet and juicy, so delicious.Lychee was a very precious fruit in their world. Even the royal family could only eat it a few times a year, and ordinary people had never even heard of the name of this fruit.She was lucky enough to taste one, and the taste still remains in her memory.But compared to the lychee I just ate, the one I tasted a long time ago didn't taste good at all. It's not too sweet and tastes astringent, so she has never been interested in fruits like lychees.Seeing that she was very satisfied with the lychees, the vendor continued to sell them hard. Girl, I'm not lying to you. Isn't this lychee very sweet It has the flavor of cinnamon. It has just been put on the market. If you want it, I will give it to you cheaper.Cinnamon flavorSeeing that she didn't understand, the vendor explained: This is a variety of lychee. It tastes very sweet and has a bit of osmanthus aroma.Bai Xiangning suddenly realized it, and then said to the vendor: I want all of these, please help me weigh them.Want them allThe vendor didn't expect that there was no business all morning, but a big customer came as soon as he arrived. All his lychees added up to ten or twenty kilograms. If they were all sold out, he would be able to close the stall early today. restHe smiled broadly, took a big bag and put all the lychees in it. After Bai Xiangning paid the money, he took the initiative and said: Girl, this bag is so heavy, how about I help You can take it backBai Xiangning was worried. When the vendor said this, she pointed in the direction of the small restaurant and said: Please help me send it there.Okay, I guarantee it will be delivered to you in good condition.After arriving at the door and seeing the sign of the small restaurant, the vendor thought to herself, it turns out that this girl runs a restaurant. No wonder she ordered so many lychees at once. How could ordinary people buy so many kilosBut he was a little confused. Even if he ran a restaurant, how could he use so many lycheesCan you use lychees for cookingHe thought about it over and over, but couldn't think of any reason, so he simply stopped thinking about it. Anyway, all the lychees were sold, and what the customers wanted to use them for was not his concern.In fact, his guess was correct. Bai Xiangning was indeed planning to use lychees to create a new product.

Chapter 22Qiao Ping opened the door and came in, and saw a basket on the table filled with fresh lychees.She stepped forward and weighed it with her hands. It was very heavy, probably weighing more than twenty kilograms.She said to herself: Why did Boss Bai buy so many lycheesAt this time, Bai Xiangning came out of the kitchen and said to Qiao Ping: I just bought this this morning. You can taste it.Qiao Ping took one. This lychee was different from the ones she had eaten before. It was small and the skin was a little prickly, but the color looked very red.Is this delicious Qiao Ping was a little skeptical.But after peeling one open and putting it in her mouth, Qiao Ping immediately retracted her previous thoughts.This lychee is so delicious, rightShe shouldn't doubt Boss Bai's taste. How has Boss Bai ever made a mistakeSeeing her expression, Bai Xiangning knew that she must like to eat, so she said: "Take more and taste it, I will buy more."Qiao Ping picked up another lychee. Although this lychee was not big, it had a thin skin and a flat and small core. The flesh was plump, crispy and sweet. When you bite it gently, the sweet and fragrant juice will be in your mouth. It explodes in my mouth and is so sweet that it reaches my heart.Unlike a variety she had eaten before, the part near the core was very astringent, this time the lychee pulp was sweet from the inside to the outside, and there was a faint unique aroma inside.I happened to see someone selling this kind of lychees on my way to the vegetable market this morning, so I bought them all. The vendor selling lychees told me that this variety is called Guiwei, so named because of the fragrance of osmanthus.Qiao Ping suddenly realized, why does it taste like osmanthusThen she asked doubtfully: But Boss Bai, what did you buy so many lychees forOf course she wouldn't think that Boss Bai bought it back to give her something to eat. There must be other uses for it.The weather has been getting hotter and hotter recently, so I plan to use this lychee to make an ice drink. She pulled Qiao Ping to a chair and sat down, smiling and saying: "We have been busy all morning."These lychees can't be used up at one time. She plans to peel a few kilograms first, put the rest in the refrigerator, and take them out tomorrow.But even if it is only a few kilograms, it will take a long time to peel it off.Bai Xiangning brought over the largest white porcelain bowl in the store to put the lychee pulp.Qiao Ping had already begun to peel the lychee, but she couldn't get it right. The skin of the peeled flesh was pitted and the juice ran down her hands.Oops, Qiao Ping is a little annoyed. How can she use the lychees after she peeled them like thisBai Xiangning said: Don't worry, watch me peel it off first.In fact, the lychee is easy to peel. Although the skin is a little prickly, there is an obvious seam in the middle. If you pinch it gently along the seam, the skin of the lychee will split in half, revealing the pulp inside. Come.Bai Xiangning demonstrated to Qiao Ping that the pulp would not be damaged at all and it was easy to peel.Qiao Ping tried it again, and the peeled pulp was much better than before.She said in surprise: Boss Bai, you are so smart. It won't be troublesome at all to peel it off like this.In fact, I didn't know how to do it at first, but I got the hang of it after peeling off a few more.Bai Xiangning went to the kitchen and got two pairs of food-grade latex gloves. The lychees were used to make ice drinks, so wearing gloves could avoid touching the pulp. Besides, the skin of lychees can prick your hands, so peeling off just one or two is fine. They have to peel so many, and if they don't wear gloves, their hands will probably be pricked and hurt by then.The latex gloves fit the fingers very well, so wearing them did not affect the movements. Qiao Ping felt that she could peel lychees faster with the gloves on.After mastering the correct method and having the tools at hand, Bai Xiangning and Qiao Ping peeled all the lychees they needed in less than an hour and filled a large porcelain bowl.Okay, let's peel off this much first.Bai Xiangning picked up the bowl and walked to the kitchen. She will now officially start making lychee ice drink.Ten minutes later, Bai Xiangning handed a glass of drink to Qiao Ping, please try it and see if it tastes good.Qiao Ping happily accepted it. She has been working with Boss Bai ever since. Every time a new product is released, she can be the first to taste it. She is so happy.Baixiangning is served in a transparent glass. The ice drink inside is light in color and looks particularly delicious and refreshing.Qiao Ping took a small sip first, and then couldn't help but take a big sip.It had the texture of a smoothie, and you could still taste the lychee pulp at the end of the drink, which was cold and sweet. Qiao Ping quickly drank the whole glass.tastyQiao Ping nodded heavily. It tasted so good. It tasted like the natural sweetness of lychee and was not greasy at all.Bai Xiangning named this new product Lychee Ice Jasmine. The main raw materials are cinnamon-flavored lychee and jasmine tea. After her blending, the two were perfectly blended together.The elective course teacher was giving an impassioned lecture on the stage, while He Peng was scrolling through his cell phone boredly.There was no air conditioning in the classroom, so he was too weak to even browse the video. His chin rested on his left arm, and his other hand kept swiping at the screen of his mobile phone.It's really boring. None of the videos pushed to him are of interest to him.Just when he was about to close the software, a small red dot suddenly appeared in the upper right corner, indicating that the users he followed had posted new videos.His account only followed one user, and that was the video account of Bai Family Restaurant. He was excited and immediately clicked in. Sure enough, it was a new video released by Bai Family Restaurant.The title is very concise, the new restaurant has lychee ice jasmineLychee Ice JasmineThe name sounds pretty good. It should be something like a cold drink.He Peng clicked on the video. Just two seconds after watching it, his mouth was dry. This new product looked delicious and made him thirsty. He wanted to buy a drink now.Since the last time Bai Xiangning registered a video account, Bai Xiangning has worked hard to make more attractive videos.Every night after the restaurant closes, she takes time to practice shooting videos. After practicing for a while, the videos she shoots start to look good.This new product video is the first video that was actually made by her. She shot it over and over again several times and finally got a more satisfactory version.Sure enough, once it was released, the number of views immediately increased.The video is not long, about two minutes, and shows the super beauty of Lychee Ice Jasmine in all directions, making everyone who watches the video want to rush to a small restaurant and order a drink.After He Peng watched the video, there was only one thought left in his mind, that is, he must drink lychee ice jasmine today. No one can stop him.After Bai Xiangning released the video, she also announced the news to her customer base simultaneously, "Dang Dang Dang Dang, the restaurant has a new product. Let a cup of lychee iced jasmine cool you down throughout the hot summer."Then she attached a link to the video she just uploaded.After she sent this message, the people below immediately screamed again and again.Ah, what did I see Boss Bai said that the restaurant has a new one.Woo hoo hoo, it' s not in vain. I look forward to the stars and the moon every day, and finally the new product of the small restaurant is here.After Bai Xiangning sent the video link to this large group of thousands of people, the number of views of the video increased sharply.After the group friends came back after watching the video.Ahhhhh, this new product looks great. Although I haven' t drank it yet, I declare it to be the most delicious drink.Oh my god, does the appearance of this ice drink really exist In terms of appearance, it is not even inferior to those of the white bosses of specialized milk tea shops. They are too versatile. They can do everything.Woohoo, I'm still working hard in class, can I still drink a nice glass of lychee iced jasmine after class The person who sent the message continued to cry, if I can't drink lychee iced jasmine today, my Spirit, some of my beautiful and good characters can no longer be preserved. WuwuwuThat's an exaggeration upstairs, it's just a glass of iced drink, it's not that bad.Bai Xiangning edited another message and sent it, lychee iced jasmine, 10 yuan a cup, limited to 30 cups today.Since it was a fresh taste, Bai Xiangning did not prepare too much. She needed to decide how much to make next based on customer feedback. If you make a lot at the beginning, if customers don't like it, it will cause waste.It's not that she doesn't have confidence in her craft, it's just that as a restaurant owner, she has to be more cautious.Every ingredient is hard-earned, so Bai Xiangning will try to avoid wasting it. What's more, this time she and Qiao Ping peeled the lychees one by one. She would be heartbroken to waste any of them.The lychees peeled today were enough to make thirty cups of iced drinks. Bai Xiangning did the math and felt that thirty cups should be enough to sell out.When the small restaurant opened in the evening, He Peng was the first to rush in.Boss Bai, take a glass of lychee iced jasmine first.He Peng ran all the way over, panting, and his heart almost jumped out of his throat.He asked Bai Xiangning nervously: Is there moreHe skipped his elective class again and rushed here without stopping. He should be able to drink the lychee iced jasmine he had been thinking about all afternoon.Seeing his cautious look, Bai Xiangning laughed. She quickly took a glass from the counter and handed it to him. There are many. You are the first to take a sip to cool down.After getting the lychee ice jasmine, He Peng's heart fell back to its original position.It seems that he is quite fast, and he was the first to drink the new product. Hey, hey, he will try it now.The lychee iced jasmine is made by Bai Xiangning. There is a little smoothie in it. The ice is so cold that the walls of the cup are soaked with water droplets.He Peng just ran in from outside. He was so hot that he was covered in sweat. He couldn't help but take a big sip.Ah, a refreshing coolness flowed through his internal organs, and the heat subsided a lot.Boss, is jasmine tea added to this It tastes like a faint jasmine fragrance.Yes, the main raw materials of this ice drink are lychee and jasmine tea.He Peng praised: Boss Bai, you are so awesome. Not only do you make delicious food, but you also make delicious drinks.Bai Xiangning smiled and rolled her eyes, haha, you can drink it if you like.He Penggudonggudong drank a glass quickly. He blinked and said to Bai Xiangning: Boss Bai, can you give me another glassBefore Bai Xiangning could reply, a voice of opposition came from outside the door: No, you have already had a drink. Can you leave the opportunity to those of us who haven' t had a drinkThat' s right, boss, please limit it to one drink per person.Boss, I'll be here as soon as I get off work. Please let me drink lychee iced jasmine, otherwise I won't have the motivation to go to work tomorrow.bossBai Xiangning looked at the long queue outside and said to He Peng in embarrassment: Why don't you come back and buy it tomorrow The quantity today is not much, and one person can only buy one cup.He Peng was very disappointed. The glass just now was not enough at all.But looking at the people still waiting in line outside, He Peng felt comfortable again, and a little proud.Hey hey hey, he is the first one to drink lychee ice jasmine Oh, envy, envyHe puffed up his chest and walked out struttingly in the envious eyes of everyone, as if he was afraid that he had not attracted enough hatred.Ha ha ha haHe will buy it again tomorrow and have a drink every dayYe Chenge was selected to join the school's choir last week. She has been dragged to rehearse every afternoon these past few days. She has been practicing all afternoon, and her voice is almost hoarse.But it happened that she was preparing for the centenary anniversary of the school. Even if her throat hurt, she had to persevere.In two days, it will be the day to officially perform on stage. Once it gets over, she will feel completely relaxed.Ahem. Her throat was so itchy that Ye Chenge couldn't help coughing twice. Her best friend immediately patted her back and said worriedly: Chenge, are you okayYe Chenge cleared his throat and said: It's okay, I'll just drink some water.My best friend frowned and complained: It's true that the school drags you to rehearse. They don't even prepare a bottle of water on the field. You can only drink water after rehearsing every time. Whose throat can bear it if this goes onIt doesn't matter, it will be over in two days.My best friend thought of something, took out her phone, clicked on a video and put it in front of Ye Chenge.Morning song, look at itWhat is this Ye Chenge curiously leaned over to take a look, and then his attention was attracted by the refreshing and cold-looking drink in the video.It seemed to be delicious. Ye Chenge couldn't help but swallow the water. What was going on She suddenly felt very thirsty. She had just drank a large glass of water.How's it going Does it look good Why don't you go and drink itAh, is this a newly opened milk tea shop Is it not far from hereYe Chenge wanted to ask again, but was interrupted by his best friend. Let's go to the store first. This new product is limited to thirty cups. If you go late, there will be no more.This newly opened milk tea shop is limited to 30 cups and actually engages in hunger marketingYe Chenge was confused. Before he had time to think about it, his best friend dragged him to a small restaurant.When he arrived at the door, Ye Chenge looked at the conspicuous sign above: Bai Family Restaurant, and turned to look at his best friend in confusion.This is the little restaurant you want to take me toShe thought that the good-looking and delicious drink in the video came from some new milk tea shop, but it turned out that it came from a restaurant.How good can a drink made by a restaurant be Isn't it just a publicity stuntHer throat was already uncomfortable enough, and it would definitely be even more uncomfortable if she drank something with some added flavoring and saccharin.Ye Chenge immediately lost the idea of trying. Her throat was already tortured, and she couldn't cause it any more damage.Forget it, I don't really want to drink this. Why don't you go buy it and I'll wait for you outside.No, come with me. My best friend pointed to the queue in front of me and said, "Look how hard it is for us to get in line. It would be a pity not to buy a drink."That, that's fine. Ye Chenge said reluctantly.Since your best friend wants to drink it so much, then just buy a drink with her. She has made up her mind not to drink it anyway.After a while.Ye Chenge held the straw in his mouth and drank lychee ice jasmine one after another.I thought, it smells so good.

Chapter 23They arrived just in time to catch the last two drinks.Ye Chenge really didn't want to buy it at first, but when they were waiting in line, the ice drink on the counter immediately hit her heart.It actually looks better than the one in the video. The transparent cup allows you to clearly see the drink inside. The warm jasmine tea blends with the cold lychee, crystal clear, and there seems to be some suet-fat jade underneath. of pulp.Ye Chenge's heart moved shamefully.Her best friend knew that she didn't want to buy it, so she said to Xiang Ning: Boss, I want a glass of lychee iced jasmine.Two cups.The best friend looked at Ye Chenge in surprise, who just said she would never drink itYe Chenge turned a blind eye to his best friend's questioning eyes.Even though I'm here, I can't say why I don't want to buy a drink.She held the lychee ice jasmine in her hand and felt a chill on her fingertips. Ye Chenge inserted the straw in and took a sip, his eyes suddenly brightened.Wow, deliciousShe and her best friend said at the same time.Seeing how drunk she was, her best friend couldn't help but joke: Didn't you just say that you would never drinkYe Chenge: I didn't say. She would never admit it.She lowered her head and took another sip. The taste of the lychee iced jasmine was completely different from what she had imagined. It tasted exactly like the original taste of lychee, without the added flavor she thought it had.After one sip, the dry and itchy throat was relieved and became less uncomfortable.WellAfter taking a few sips, the straw was suddenly blocked by something. Ye Chenge took a hard sip and sucked up a few lychee pulps. She chewed them, and the sweet juice full of cinnamon flavor flowed into her mouth, giving her a few more points. surprise.Why is this lychee so sweetThe pulp tastes crunchy and juicy, making people want to suck in the sweetness of the pulp.Ye Chenge quickly drank half the cup.When my best friend saw this, she said: It turns out that my eyesight is pretty good, rightYe Chenge laughed and said: You are the bestShe continued, "I didn't have any hope before I came here. After all, no one thinks that cold drinks made in a restaurant can taste that good." But when I took my first bite, I realized how wrong I was. The products of this small restaurant are even better than most milk tea shops.My best friend agreed with her opinion, that is, there was a new milk tea shop opened next to our school. We had to wait in line for more than an hour, but after drinking it, our mouths were filled with the taste of saccharin, which was overwhelming.Don't mention it. I felt sticky in my mouth after drinking it. I felt so uncomfortable. Ye Chenge took another sip of pulp and said vaguely: "It's not like this. It's very comfortable to drink. The mouthful is filled with the natural sweetness of lychees." .She shook the half-empty cup in her hand and sighed: 10 yuan a cup is still real material, what a bargain.My best friend nodded, but unfortunately it was limited to thirty cups and today's portion has been sold out.As soon as she finished speaking, a scream suddenly came from beside her.Ah ah ah, it's sold out. I hurry up and hurry up, but I still can't catch upAh, God knows how much I paid for this drink. My legs are almost broken.A young man in his early twenties was bent over, holding his hands on his knees and panting violently, looking extremely tired.There were several customers following him, all of whom came specifically to buy lychee ice jasmine. When they learned that it was sold out, their faces showed obvious disappointment.Some of them are students who have just finished class, and some are workers who have just finished their jobs. They have been thinking about it for an afternoon, and they rely on this to survive.Ye Chenge and his best friend looked at each other, secretly glad that they came earlier and did not miss such delicious lychee ice jasmine, otherwise they would be one of those sighing now.Bai Xiangning felt a little embarrassed when she saw several customers in the back disappointed because they didn't buy the iced drink they were longing for.She originally expected to sell only thirty cups, but the actual situation exceeded her expectations. All thirty cups were sold out in less than twenty minutes.She said apologetically: I'm really sorry for causing everyone to make this trip in vain. I have prepared relatively few new products today, but I will prepare more tomorrow.After saying that, she added that there is also iced mung bean soup in the store. Customers who haven't bought it can try it. It is also very good at relieving the heat.There's also mung bean soup. Give me a cup, then.I just had her mung bean soup two days ago, and it was delicious. It only cost 2 yuan, which is a great deal.At this time, the customer in front had already drank the ice-cold mung bean soup. Ah, it was so refreshing. After taking a sip of the mung bean soup, I suddenly felt less uncomfortable. I didn't get any new products today, so come early tomorrow.After saying that, he left leisurely with mung bean soup in his hands.There are still more than ten kilograms of lychees left in the refrigerator. Based on the lesson learned the day before, Bai Xiangning plans to use all the lychees to make ice drinks this time.Early the next morning, she and Qiao Ping sat in the shop and started peeling lychees.They peeled more lychees, and their speed became faster and faster. They peeled all the lychees and put them in the bowl before lunch.Phew, finally finished peeling it offBai Xiangning kept her head down and concentrated on peeling the shells. Bai Xiangning felt that her neck was about to break. Even though I was wearing latex gloves, my fingers still hurt a little from being poked. Without the gloves, my fingers would probably be broken by now.Qiao Ping was also a little tired, but she didn't say anything. She just put the bowl full of lychee pulp in the refrigerator.I used up all the remaining lychees today, and the white fragrance made me want to go buy some more to prepare.She walked to the place where she bought lychees last time, and sure enough she saw the vendor sitting on a pony, concentrating on arranging the lychees in front of her.Bai Xiangning walked over.Hello, I'm here to buy lychees again.The vendor looked up, oh, the big customer is here again.He hurriedly said: I just bought these lychees this morning. How much do you wantDid you sell it here this morning Bai Xiangning looked at the basket in front of him. It was still almost full, and hardly any were sold.The vendor smiled awkwardly, yes, he came early in the morning, but no one came to ask, let alone buy.This cinnamon flavor is sold well in other places, but people here don't like to buy it. They think the fruit is too small and the shell is prickly, so my business here is far inferior to other stores. The vendor sighed as he spoke, "Hey, if I didn't grow this at home, I would have switched to selling other fruits."Bai Xiangning caught the key word, do you think this is what you grow at homeyesIf I want a large quantity, can you give me the wholesale priceYesterday, Lychee Ice Jasmine was very popular with customers as soon as it was launched, completely exceeding her expectations. Bai Xiangning felt that this ice drink could continue to be sold throughout the summer. In this case, the amount of cinnamon-flavored lychee needed would be very large.Bai Xiangning has also observed in the past two days. There is only this stall nearby selling cinnamon-flavored lychees, and no one else sells it.She also bought other varieties of lychees to try, but the finished products were not as effective as the cinnamon-flavored ones. After thinking about it, she decided to continue using cinnamon-flavored ones.If there is a stable supply channel, it will be much easier for her to purchase goods later.Of course you can. If you purchase goods from me for a long time, I will definitely give you the lowest price.The vendor smiled so hard that his eyes narrowed to slits. The last time Bai Xiangning bought all the lychees from him, he had a hunch that this was a big customer. His guess was indeed right.Then the quality can be guaranteed, rightThe vendor patted his chest and reassured her: Don't worry, the quality of my lychees cannot be overstated. You should know that they are all plump after buying them once.OK, as long as the quality is guaranteed, there will be no problem.In fact, even if Bai Xiangning didn't take the initiative, the vendors would not sell defective products to Bai Xiangning. When he went to deliver the goods last time, he already knew that Bai Xiangning owned a restaurant, and restaurants had a large purchase volume. Only stable quality could make others willing to cooperate with him for a long time.He would not be so stupid as to lose this big customer for temporary gain.Bai Xiangning and the vendor quickly agreed on the price, and they also exchanged contact information. If Bai Xiangning needs to purchase goods later, she only needs to tell the vendor in advance, and he will deliver the goods to her door.Then please send these to my store.

Chapter 24At noon, a large number of starving office workers would pour out of the office building, and the surrounding restaurants would be swept away like locusts passing by.It doesn't matter whether it tastes good or not, as long as it can fill the stomach. They are social animals and are not particular about it.Of course, the main reason is that you don't have to pay attention to it. There is no innovation in the nearby stores. They just cook the same dishes all day and eat for a few days. It's okay. People like them who have worked for several years have already eaten all around. , the sense of taste is numb.Zhou Fei, why don't you go down to eatWhen a colleague passed by, he saw that Zhou Fei had no intention of getting up and going downstairs, so he asked strangely.Zhou Fei raised his head, his face was very sad, and even his lips were bloodless.Colleagues were shocked, what's wrong with youZhou Fei closed his eyes and said with a painful look on his face: Damn, I'm so unlucky. I ordered a takeaway at noon yesterday and started having diarrhea after eating. I almost didn't sleep all night last night and ran to the toilet all the time.Oops, which kind of illegal store is this I must report it.He then asked in a low voice: "Well, you won't eat at noon today, do you want me to go down and bring you something"Zhou Fei was listless, his head drooped on the table. When he heard his colleague's words, he just shook his head to express that he didn't want to eat.Seeing this, my colleague said helplessly: Hey, to be honest, I don't want to eat it either. I eat that every day and it makes me want to vomit. I don't know what kind of oil is in that dish. I'll get sick of it after just a few bites, but there's nothing I can do if I don't eat it. I have no other choice at noon.He lost the urge to eat after what he said, so he simply sat next to Zhou Fei and continued chatting. However, the shop below could at least see it. Those takeaways were really eaten blindfolded. Who could Do you know what kind of environment it was made fromZhou Fei groaned and said: "That's right, after suffering this disaster, I will never dare to order takeout again. The price I paid is too high."He then said to his colleagues: It's a pity that Bai's small restaurant is only open in the evening. If you said it was open at noon, I wouldn't have to worry about where to eat now.Yes, Bai's Little Restaurant is definitely our first choice.The two of them sighed at the same time. When can we have food from the small restaurant at noonZhou Fei can be regarded as an old customer of the Bai Family Small Restaurant. He tried it not long after it opened, and many of his colleagues also successfully fell into the trap of the small restaurant.After eating the food in the small restaurant, I feel uncomfortable eating in other restaurants.What is this calledI could have endured the darkness if I had never seen the light.If they have never eaten in a restaurant as delicious as a small restaurant, then they can continue to endure the terrible takeout and the boring fast food downstairs.But now that they have Bai Yueguang in their hearts, it will be very painful to go to other restaurants.Zhou Fei took out the bread that he had treasured for a long time (and forgotten for a long time) from the drawer, tore open the package, and stuffed it into his mouth with a numb expression.Don't ask for good food, just ask for food.And, stop having diarrhea. His fragile belly really couldn't withstand any trauma anymore.Finally, after a painful afternoon, the hands of the clock on the office wall pointed to six o'clock.Zhou Fei picked up his backpack and ran away, completely missing his half-dead look in the afternoon.Bai's small restaurant, he's hereWhat do you want to eat todayFacing this regular customer, Bai Xiangning showed a big smile.One each of mapo tofu, sweet and sour eggplant, three cups of chicken, plum and pork ribs, and a cup of lychee and iced jasmineBai Xiangning looked behind him and asked hesitantly: "How many of you are eating together"No, I'm the only one eating it.Bai Xiangning was silent for a moment, and then said: My appetite is quite good today.Not only is it good, but one person can eat so much. Can the reincarnation of the Big Eater eat it allHowever, she just thought about this in her heart and did not say it out loud. After all, every customer has his own idea. Maybe this customer planned to pack it up and take it back.Zhou Fei said with a naive smile: I am really hungry today.He was holding his breath just to go to a small restaurant after work to save his life. But he had to work hard all day by ordering a few more dishes. Of course he had to treat himself well after get off work.After all the dishes were served, Zhou Fei began to inhale the storm.The eggplant is delicious, crispy on the outside and tender on the inside; the mapo tofu is quite spicy when eaten, and the spicy taste is so exciting that it is so exciting; the plum pork ribs make him salivate like crazy when he eats them. The appetite is even more heightened. At this time, I want to have a piece of delicious three-cup chicken. It can't be too perfect.His stomach was like a bottomless pit, and those few dishes entered his stomach in minutes.When he drank the last of the lychee ice jasmine, Bai Xiangning was stunned.If it weren't for the fact that Zhou Fei didn't have a camera in front of him, she would really have thought that some big eater was doing the live broadcast.Zhou Fei was finally full. The satisfaction that the small restaurant brought him was unmatched by any restaurant outside. He let out a sigh of happiness, and then suddenly remembered something, so while he was white Xiang Ning was not busy, walked to her side and said:Boss Bai, have you considered opening at noonOpen from noonBai Xiangning naturally thought about it. If it was also open at noon, the revenue of the small restaurant would be higher, but it would also be busier.According to the current customer flow of the small restaurant, she and Qiao Ping can barely cope with it, but if it opens at noon, it will not be enough for them to be the only ones in the store, and more manpower will be needed.In fact, some customers have asked her this question before, but she got over it with a slap in the face.Recently, more and more people have asked, and many customers have also asked in the group. Once someone initiates this topic, the number of messages that follow immediately becomes 99+. Everyone is looking forward to the Baijia small restaurant at noon. Open for business.Bai Xiangning couldn't ignore Zhou Fei's expectant eyes, but she couldn't immediately give a positive answer. She could only say: There are not enough people in the store at the moment. When suitable people are recruited, we will consider lunch. Business.That's great. Zhou Fei is about to jump with excitement. Boss Bai has said so, which means that there is a high possibility that the small restaurant will open at noon. Then he will no longer have to worry about noon. What did you eatHis pitiful stomach finally no longer has to suffer the poisonous hand of takeaways and can be relieved.Bai Xiangning didn't know what he was thinking of, but she always felt that when he left, there were many happy bubbles on his head.After closing at night, Bai Xiangning lay on the bed and seriously thought about the issue of opening at noon.Lack of manpower is the biggest obstacle.She rolled over and turned on the system.The system, which had been left out for a long time, immediately cleverly opened the points mall, without Bai Xiangning even speaking.She has accumulated a lot of points now, and a reliable helper only costs 500, which is no problem for her now.etc.Bai Xiangning looked at the interface in front of her and began to doubt her eyes.Why did something that originally only cost 500 points become 5,000 What is this black heart mallSensing that the host was in a bad mood, the system explained obediently: The points spent on purchasing the same item again will be doubled ten times.Bai Xiangning immediately wanted to close the points mall interface.The system quickly stopped him: Wait, wait, wait, you can choose what kind of helper you want this time.

Chapter 25Several options immediately appeared in front of Bai Xiangning.Helpers with past kitchen experience will receive +1,000 points.A helper with good looks and good temperament will get +1000 points.A helper who works quickly and quickly will get +1000 points.Bai Xiangning asked: Can I choose more than onesure.Although this points mall is very dark, this time it gives her a choice. She can find a more suitable helper according to her own needs. The price is more expensive. Anyway, she still has points saved now. Quite a few.It is very important to have previous kitchen experience, so check it.Good looks and good temperament are not necessary conditions. After all, catering is not a talent show. As long as you have the appearance of a normal person, it is enough. Don't choose this.Being quick and quick as a clerk is also a must-choice.Bai Xiangning thought for a moment and finally chose the first and third options.The host needs to pay a total of 7,000 points.Okay, it will be debited directly from my account. Bai Xiangning said arrogantly, she is no longer the cash-strapped person she was before.Although she spent a lot of points this time, she believed she could earn them back soon.With the experience of recruiting people for the first time, Bai Xiangning was not in a hurry this time. She knew that the selected helper would appear in her store sooner or later.Where is the soup that made you drink last nightFang Xin walked into the kitchen, but when he opened the soup bucket, he found that it was empty. Only some water drops that had not dried after washing were left awkwardly on the wall of the bucket.Seeing him getting angry, the other helpers didn't dare to speak.Then another chef came over, patted him on the shoulder and said with a smile: What's wrong Why are you making such a big fussFang Xin looked at the person in front of him, his mood was extremely bad, but he still held back his emotions and said: Yesterday I asked them to make the soup for today, but these guys turned a deaf ear to my words and made no preparations. How can we make vegetables without stockThe more he talked, the angrier he became, and in the end he couldn't help but slapped the table hard, which frightened the other workers into shrinking their shoulders and lowering their heads and saying nothing.The man next to him smiled and said: I thought it was some big deal. I don't have any stock. I have it here. Just use this to mix it. The taste is not much different.Fang Xin took a look and saw that he was holding a bottle in his hand. On the bottle was written XXX brand concentrated soup, and there was a line of small words at the bottom, allowing you to enjoy delicious soup without any effort.The slogan is quite good.But as a time-honored restaurant, how could they fool their customers with something like thisSeeing Liu Wangfei nonchalantly preparing to mix the soup with the semi-finished product in his hand, Fang Xin strode over with his hand in front of him and said sternly: If you do this, does the store manager knowLiu Wangfei chuckled, but there was a trace of contempt in his eyes. Who do you think ordered me to do thisHe waved away Fang Xin's hand that was blocking him, poured the concentrated broth into the pot calmly, and then directed the helper next to him to add water. After a while, the aroma started to rise.You see, after all the hard work of making the soup the night before, I had it ready in two minutes. He looked Fang Xin up and down, and then said slowly and leisurely, you are just too old-fashioned and don't know how to keep pace with the times. There are more labor-saving ways, so why do you have to work so hardyou youFang Xin never expected that Liu Wangfei would be so arrogant and dare to use such a semi-finished product openly under his noseHe wanted to ask more questions, but when he thought of what Liu Wangfei had just said, his voice lowered, and he confirmed with Liu Wangfei almost pleadingly: You just said that it was our store manager who ordered you to do this. madeOf course, without his consent, I wouldn't dare to do it even if I had a hundred courages.The concentrated broth has been completely integrated into the water, and the fragrance lingers in the kitchen, surrounding Fang Xin's entire body. It is obviously a fragrance, but it is nauseating.At this time, the store manager heard the commotion and came to the kitchen.Seeing that Fang Xin and Liu Wangfei were at war with each other, he came over to smooth things over.He patted Fang Xin, who looked depressed, and said to him seriously: Fang Xin, you have been coming to Wei Ding Ji for a long time. You should know that this is all for the sake of the hotel manager. long-term development considerations. Now store costs and labor costs are increasing. If we don't reduce the cost of ingredients, how can our store continue to operateFang Xin murmured: But we are Wei Ding Ji, a time-honored brand in Jinghua City. We built our brand name bit by bit based on taste. If we use these concentrated soup stock, how can we be worthy of supporting and trusting us all the time Isn't this a sign of customers damaging their own signWhat he said was so sincere that he even made the store manager laugh, thinking that there are still such honest and silly boys these days.But he just thought about this in his heart, and still pretended to be sincere on his face. He continued to reason with Fang Xin nicely, "You, you just think too much, you really think that the customers outside can tell..." Come on, what kind of ingredients do we use What they eat is the same brand. As long as it is produced by our Wei Dingji, they will accept it in full.Liu Wangfei, including the helpers in the kitchen, all have the same expressions as the store manager. Only Fang Xin here is a different kind of existence.He thought it was all ridiculous.When he first came to Wei Ding Ji to work as a chef, he took a fancy to the signature here and felt that he could grow and experience himself here. He has always worked hard to make satisfying food for customers.To this end, he devoted all his time and energy, constantly honing his cooking skills, just so that customers would feel satisfied from the bottom of their hearts when eating the food he made by himself.In fact, he had already noticed that Wei Ding Ji was different from before.Nowadays, Wei Dingji has branches all over Jinghua City, and its reputation is so great that even the neighboring city has heard of the name of Wei Dingji.Whether it's a company annual meeting, a family New Year's Eve dinner, or a gathering of any size, everyone's first choice is Wei Ding Ji.Under the pursuit and support of many customers, Wei Dingji has long lost its original intention.In the past, the store manager would go to all the vegetable and farmer markets in Jinghua City in order to find the freshest ingredients. He would also drag them to experiment again and again in order to find the best seasoning ratio for the dishes, in order to satisfy the customers. Keep the sense of surprise and constantly introduce creative dishes.But now, the store manager told him that customers can't tell what ingredients they use. As long as it is produced by Wei Dingji, customers will take all orders.So even if they start using semi-finished pre-made products, it doesn't matter anymoreFang Xin was disheartened. He knew that this was no longer a place he wanted to continue fighting for.After all the customers in the store left, Bai Xiangning and Qiao Ping started to pack the tables and chairs and clean up.There was a squeak.The door was pushed open.Sorry, we are already closed.Fang Xin suddenly woke up and realized that he had actually walked into a closed store. What was he thinkingHe apologized quickly: I'm sorry, I'm sorry, I went in the wrong direction. I'll leave now.He turned around and was about to leave, but his stomach made an extremely loud noise.Fang Xin:After Wei Dingji left, he was in a state of despair and kept wandering around without even bothering to eat. I obviously didn't feel anything before, so why am I screaming nowYou haven't eaten yetBai Xiangning stopped him.Although it was already closed, this person looked extremely depressed, and he didn't know what kind of blow he had just experienced.It's so late, and there's nothing to eat outside. He would be even more sad if I didn't give him something to eat.Fang Xin held his stomach miserably, fearing that it would bark at an inappropriate time again. When Bai Xiangning asked, he replied: "I haven't eaten."Bai Xiangning said: All the dishes in the store have been sold out. If you don't mind, I will go to the kitchen to order some noodles for you now.Fang Xin quickly said: "I don't mind. I don't mind. I can just do anything."He has good intentions, so he definitely can't be picky. It's so late, so it would be nice to have something to eat.Seeing that Fang Xin was still a little cautious, Qiao Ping said to him: Sit down quickly, you are so hungry, and you have no strength to stand.Fang Xin quickly found a seat and sat down.After sitting down, he looked at the environment in the store. Although the store was not large, even a bit too small compared to the size of Wei Dingji occupying the same building, it was very clean. , the tables and chairs are neatly arranged, making people feel very comfortable there.Bai Xiangning quickly walked up to Fang Xin with a bowl of noodles. She knew that Fang Xin was hungry and was afraid that he wouldn't be full, so she packed it in a large noodle bowl.Fang Xin took it with both hands and thanked him repeatedly.You're welcome, eat it while it's hot.The ingredients for the small restaurant are basically bought in the morning that day, so at night there is nothing left in the shop, so Bai Xiangning cooks the noodles with the broth that has been simmering in the pot over low heat.Previously, I used the middle part of fresh pork ribs to make Hua Mei Spare Ribs, but Bai Xiangning used all the parts on both sides to make soup.The carefully brewed bone soup makes a bowl of plain noodles become flavorful. The taste of the soup is not very strong, but it is long and long-lasting, making people feel warm.Fang Xin picked up the bowl and took a big sip of the soup. The soup, which concentrated the essence of the bones, was mellow and moist, sliding down his throat like silk.The noodles are cooked separately and then put into the bone broth, so they taste refreshing and chewy, with no soup mixed at all.Fang Xin's forehead was covered with sweat after eating. Seeing this, Bai Xiangning thoughtfully lowered the temperature of the air conditioner. Fang Xin felt the change in the surrounding temperature. It was cooler outside, but he felt warm inside. What a mess.He didn't expect that he could eat such a bowl of noodles this late at night, and every bite made him feel extremely happy.In his mind, roadside shops like this only use semi-finished products, but they served a bowl of bone soup noodles that were filled with care. He has been a chef for so long, and after one sip, he knew that it was definitely a carefully crafted bowl. The soup that is cooked and blended does not taste that fresh at all.Why not blend it with concentrated stock That way the cost is low, and customers shouldn't be able to taste it.Fang Xin somehow managed to ask this question that had been lingering in his mind. After the words came out of his mouth, he realized that the question was really a bit offensive. Someone kindly gave him a bowl of food, but he actually asked such an outrageous question.Fang Xingang wanted to say sorry, but Bai Xiangning didn't seem to mind at all.How can customers not be able to taste it As chefs, customers can feel whether we are cooking with care or not.When she said this, her eyes were bright.

Chapter 26Fang Xin eventually became the second employee of the Bai Family Restaurant.That bowl of bone soup noodles in the middle of the night seemed to take away his soul. Since that day, Bai Xiangning could see Fang Xin in the store every day.He would come here every time when the store was not busy, find a corner seat, order a dish, and eat slowly. While eating, he was mumbling something. Bai Xiangning passed by several times and vaguely heard comments such as the sauce was authentic and the heat was good.Bai Xiangning raised her eyebrows. After these few days of observation, she seemed to already know who this person was.These eight achievements are what the system calls a helper who has experience in cooking and works neatly. Otherwise, how could he open the door of her shop by chance if there were so many shops on this streetBai Xiangning waited patiently for a few days. On the fifth day, when Fang Xin tasted all the dishes in the small restaurant, he took the initiative to find Bai Xiangning.You said you wanted to apply to be a chef hereBai Xiangning was not surprised at all. To be honest, she had been waiting for his words for a long time.Yes. Fang Xin's answer was affirmative, not like an impulsive decision at all.Yes, you can, but you need to come to the kitchen first and try out the dishes.Letting him try the dishes is also a way to get a general understanding of his craftsmanship, so that she can set her salary based on his level.Of course, no problem. I can go try the dishes now. Fang Xin is very confident in himself. He doesn't need to make any preparations and can start at any time.There are basically no customers in the store now, so Bai Xiangning let Fang Xin join the kitchen.Just use what you have on the stove and in the refrigerator. You can make whatever you want. You can do whatever you want.Fang Xin opened the refrigerator and took out a cabbage. He planned to make stir-fried cabbage.This is a very simple dish that every household can make. Fang Xin doesn't want to show off his skills. In many cases, the simplest dishes can best reflect a person's strength.Bai Xiangning leaned quietly against the kitchen door, watching Fang Xin roll up his sleeves and start tearing the cabbage.He did not cut it with a knife, but broke open the cabbage and tore it into pieces. His tearing movements were random, but the size of the torn cabbage was very even.The ingredients prepared by Fang Xin were also simple, only garlic slices, dried chili peppers, and peppercorns. After the pot started to smoke, he scooped a large spoonful of lard from the porcelain bowl next to the stove and put it into the pot.Bai Xiangning was confused. How could he act like he had been in this kitchen before Why could he know so accurately that the porcelain bowl contained lardThen she noticed the bright print on the outside of the porcelain bowl and fell into deep thought.This bowl is indeed a bowl specially made for lard.The high temperature of the pot and oil caused the aroma of the ingredients that had just been put in to quickly stir up. Fang Xin quickly poured the torn cabbage into the pot. During the whole process, the stove kept the fire on. Because of this, it was necessary to You have to act quickly, otherwise the ingredients will burn and the aroma will escape.After the cabbage was put into the pot, Fang Xin turned the pot with his left hand and stir-fried quickly with his right hand. After frying the cabbage until it was cooked through, he quickly added salt and light soy sauce, stir-fried a few more times, and then removed it from the pot. Added a little balsamic vinegar before.it is done.Fang Xin put the dishes on the plate and said to Bai Xiangning: Do you want to taste itQiao Ping poked her head out from the back of the kitchen. Just before the food was out of the pot, the aroma penetrated her nose. It was really choking, but it was also very fragrant.Bai Xiangning turned to Qiao Ping and said: Let's try it together.She took three pairs of chopsticks from the cupboard, handed one pair to Qiao Ping, and handed the other pair to Fang Xin.You made this dish and you try it too. Bai Xiangning said with a smile.As she said that, she went to pick up the vegetables.When Fang Xin took out the dish, she carefully observed that there was no excess soup under the plate and the whole dish was clean and tidy.After taking a bite, Bai Xiangning was pleasantly surprised for a moment. The new employee turned out to be more qualified than she expected.Stir-fried cabbage is not difficult to say, but if you want to make it delicious, you have to put in a lot of effort.It can be said that Fang Xin made this dish very successfully. The whole process was very hot, and the pot was full of steam. The stir-fried cabbage had an extremely crisp texture, and the numbing, spicy, and fresh aroma of the ingredients all contributed to each other. It makes the aroma of the whole dish reach an unprecedented level.Every time you take a bite, you can hear the crisp sound of the cabbage being bitten open in your mouth. The seasoning is simple, but under the rapid stir-frying at high temperature, each cabbage leaf is coated with a salty and fresh taste.Fang Xin specially added balsamic vinegar before serving it. It was only a few drops, but it was the icing on the cake, adding flavor to the whole dish. There was still a slight sourness in your mouth, adding a layer of texture.taste good. Bai Xiangning gave a very objective evaluation. She really felt that Fang Xin made this dish well.The taste of the dish exceeded her expectations, and during the cooking process, Bai Xiangning also observed carefully. Fang Xin handled the ingredients with ease, and his skillful and light handling of the pot was unparalleled in just a few years. I'm afraid I can't learn it.It seems that this time the helper has two brushes. Bai Xiangning feels that her 7,000 points are well worth the money.Now that she has tried the food and tasted it, Bai Xiangning should consider how much salary she should give her.She considered it and gave a figure. This was the average salary level of chefs in Jinghua City that she had learned about online before. On this basis, she also added some.Is this amount acceptable to youThe price Bai Xiangning gave was 9,000. She didn't know where Fang Xin worked before, so the price she gave was based entirely on what she knew.Fortunately, Fang Xin didn't say much and agreed readily.In fact, the number of 9,000 is much lower than when he was at Weidingji, but now he has a car and a house in Jinghua City, no loans, no pressure, and he has no particularly big expenses. 9,000 is enough. .What's more, in this humble little restaurant, he saw something much more expensive than 9,000 yuan.Maybe it's the original intention.

Chapter 27It's past ten o'clock in the morning, and the workers have gradually recovered from the despair of going to work at nine o'clock. They all have numb expressions and are mechanically working on the computer.In addition to the sound of frequent mouse clicks in the office, there are also curses that pop up from time to time.What's going on with Party A I've had to change a plan over ten times.Zhou Fei picked up the half-drunk Coke at hand and drank a few swigs of it angrily. The cold drink he had just taken out of the refrigerator calmed his anger a little.The colleague sitting next to him seemed to be staring at the computer intently without even turning his head, but it did not affect him in the slightest from complaining too.Don't tell me, the last time I met a stupid Party A, he asked me to change the plan more than ten times and let it go. In the end, he took away my revised plan. After looking at it, I thought the first version was the best, and decided to use the first version.He naturally took Zhou Fei's Coke and poured it into his mouth. Before Zhou Fei could protest, he continued to complain: This bitch, Party A, told me that he wanted the first version of the plan. I... If you don't, you won't have to suffer the following sinsZhou Fei said quietly: Is there a possibility that Party A hopes that the money he spends is worth it.colleague:The boss was in a meeting at this time, so Zhou Fei took out his mobile phone and started fishing with pay. When his colleagues saw this, they also took out their mobile phones and lowered their heads not knowing what they were reading.If they look to the side at this time, they will find a group of colleagues around them, none of whom are doing serious work.Zhou Fei habitually opened WeChat and pinned it to the customer group of Bai Family Restaurant. He saw a new group announcement posted there:After much consideration, Baijia Restaurant has decided to open at noon. The noon business hours are: 11:00-14:00. Thank you for your opinions and support.Also, new today: Teriyaki Chicken Leg Rice Bowl, 18 yuan/portion.Teriyaki Chicken Leg Rice Bowl.jpgBai Xiangning posted the photos she took in the group. The chicken legs wrapped in golden oily sauce were cut into long strips and neatly placed on the white crystal clear rice. Just looking at the photos You can imagine how delicious this rice bowl isDamn, Zhou Fei let out an exclamation.The colleague next to him was happily scrolling through his phone. He almost threw the phone away in fright. He immediately looked back to see if the boss was coming, but there was no one behind him.He was furious: What is your name You scared me to death.Bai's small restaurant is also open at noon. What we prayed for last time has come true. Look.Zhou Fei placed the group announcement he just saw in front of his colleagues. The suddenly enlarged font dazzled his colleagues for a moment. After he read it carefully,Damn it was exactly the same as Zhou Fei's reaction just now.And today there is also a new rice bowl. Hehehe, I have decided to eat this teriyaki chicken drumstick rice bowl.Zhou Fei almost burst into tears. He felt that he would finally be able to eat normal meals at noon.You no longer have to worry about what to eat for lunch. You can choose Baijia Restaurant without thinking.It was after ten o'clock when they saw the news, and lunch break started at twelve o'clock. They were not interested in working during the rest of the time, and they were only thinking about how fast they would rush out of the company to grab a small restaurant. Where's lunchBai Xiangning posted an announcement in the group, which means that thousands of people in the group can see the news. By noon, who knows how many competitors will compete with them.The lunch break was only so short, so he had to be fast enough so as not to waste time eating.At 11:58, Zhou Fei already had one foot towards the door, ready to sprint, waiting for 12:1 to rush out immediately.five four three two one.Time's up, go aheadBai Xiangning originally did not plan to serve new rice bowls, but most of the customers in the lunch shop are office workers nearby. Their lunch break time is limited, and rice bowls are very convenient, which can save them as much as possible. time.So she discussed it with Fang Xin and finally decided to continue selling rice bowls at noon. Of course, if customers want to order, they can still do it.Today is the first day of business at noon. Bai Xiangning and Fang Xin made Teriyaki Chicken Leg Rice Bowl for about fifty people.Bai Xiangning was busy at the counter when she suddenly felt a whirlwind blowing at the door, and then two people appeared in front of her.Zhou Fei and his colleagues had been racing all the way. He felt that if he kept running like this, it would be a matter of time before he became a long-distance running champion.Boss Bai, I want a new product, teriyaki chicken drumstick rice bowl and a glass of lychee iced jasmine.Okay, a total of 28 yuan.A colleague said: I am the same as him.After Zhou Fei and his colleagues paid, they found a seat and sat down. Phew, they could finally take a breath.This time for the Teriyaki Chicken Leg Rice Bowl, Fang Xin was responsible for frying the chicken legs in the early stages, while Bai Xiangning was responsible for adding her secret sauce until the chicken legs completely absorbed the flavor of the sauce. After that, this teriyaki chicken drumstick rice bowl is ready.Since the last agreement with the Guiwei Lychee vendor, we now have a stable supply channel for lychees, so the supply of lychee ice jasmine has also been increased to 150 cups per day, which can basically cover the customers. meet our needs.Qiao Ping walked up to Zhou Fei with a tray. The real thing of the teriyaki chicken leg rice bowl was far more impactful than the photo. The most important thing was that the overbearing fragrance emitted by the real thing was something that the photo couldn't bring.Teriyaki chicken legs are made from the most tender part of the chicken legs. After removing the bones, cut off the fascia attached to the chicken legs. This can prevent the chicken from shrinking together when frying.The skin on the surface of the chicken legs was fried until golden and crispy, and the originally fatty fat turned into a crispy shell that was fragrant and fragrant, making a crispy sound when you bite into it.Zhou Fei's eyes widened and he said excitedly to his colleagues: The skin of this chicken drumstick is so crispy.My colleague was enjoying his meal and had no time to answer him.Since the shell of the chicken leg had become extremely crispy, he pressed it lightly with a spoon, and the long strip of chicken leg meat was broken into two halves. He put the meat and rice into his mouth, and his mouth was immediately filled with A salty and sweet taste dominates, mixed with rice, making people unable to stop taking one bite after another.Chicken thigh meat is thick, but it is also the most tender part of the chicken. Although the skin is charred by high-temperature frying, the meat inside is locked in moisture, maintaining the most delicate and tender texture. One bite. The rich and plump chicken juices splash in your mouth, making you shiver with deliciousness.The sauce carefully prepared by Bai Xiangning plays a vital role in this dish.No matter how well fried the chicken legs are, the taste is bland. Only when it is wrapped in a mellow and fragrant sauce can the most delicious taste be brought out.The thick, dark brown sauce tightly wraps every inch of the chicken leg, making it look shiny and translucent under the light.

This sauce is also a perfect match for rice. Just a little bit can make the rice full of flavor. .And this full portion of teriyaki chicken legs is covered with rice, and almost every grain of rice underneath is stained with brown-red oily sauce. Stir it twice and put it in your mouth. It's indescribable. A sense of satisfaction arises spontaneously.Zhou Fei was eating when he suddenly stopped and said nonchalantly: Why does it feel like he tasted a floral fragranceMy colleague was half-full and finally had time to talk to him. He raised his head and said, "You're not mistaken. I ate it too. It must have been from sophora nectar."The specialty of his hometown is locust nectar, so he is very familiar with the smell, but he didn't dare to identify it at first, fearing that it was his own illusion. After all, the price of sophora nectar is not cheap. He did not expect that there would be merchants willing to use this kind of honey for cooking.But now even Zhou Fei has eaten it. It seems that it is not his illusion.Sophora nectar sounds like very special honey. Zhou Fei said.So his colleague gave him some popular science while eating.Zhou Fei was amazed when he heard this, and sighed: "Boss Bai is too attentive. I just said that I have eaten teriyaki chicken legs so many times at other places before, and none of them can compare with the taste this time." He scooped another big spoonful of rice and said as he ate, "Hmm, it's delicious. No wonder the sauce tastes very special and sweet. The sauce tastes great when mixed with rice. I'm going to add some more." mealWhen I looked up, I found that my colleague sitting opposite had already added rice and was now eating obliviously.Bai Xiangning also specially added some blanched vegetables next to the rice bowl, eating them alternately with the chicken thighs to relieve fatigue.Zhou Fei ate one bite of chicken and one bite of vegetables, feeling extremely happy.

Chapter 28Fang Xin was not unsurprised when he first learned that Bai Xiangning was going to use sophora nectar to make teriyaki chicken legs.During these days in the small restaurant, he thought that it was rare for Bai Xiangning to use fresh ingredients, but he did not expect that in order to improve the taste of the food, she was willing to spend such a high cost on cooking. Not to mention that honey is not the main ingredient of teriyaki chicken legs.Sophora nectar, also called acacia honey, is a very high-grade first-class honey with a light color and a unique elegant fragrance of acacia. It is not only loved by domestic consumers, but also exported to foreign countries, so the price is lower than other honeys. Honey is much higher.This is what Bai Xiangning told him at the time. Although this honey is added as the final seasoning and the amount used is not much, you should not underestimate its effect. Although ordinary honey can also be used, it is The taste of the teriyaki chicken legs is too strong. Sophora nectar has a sweet floral aroma, sweet but not greasy.

When used to make teriyaki chicken legs, it not only brings a unique flavor, but also changes the overall taste. It's light and not easy to get cloying when you eat it.Teriyaki chicken legs, a dish he had made many times when he was learning to cook, but never once did he consider the impact of the quality and variety of honey on the finished dish.Fang Xin is a serious person. After listening to what Bai Xiangning said, he bought ordinary honey for comparison.After finishing, he took a bite and put down his chopsticks with a solemn expression.How about it Bai Xiangning came over and tasted it too.Fang Xin actually admired her deeply in his heart, but on the surface he still showed some restraint. He said: You are indeed right. The sauce of the teriyaki chicken legs made with ordinary honey is too thick. It's thick and the taste is very simple. It's better to make it with sophora nectar.He has been cooking for a long time, and he has always worked very hard and conscientiously in cooking. Sometimes he is even a little too rigid, not very flexible, and lacks some creativity. When it comes to cooking, he just follows the master's instructions. He doesn't think about adding his own ideas. It turns out that most of the chefs at Wei Ding Ji were just like him, and they became rigid cooks. machine.When he came to Bai's small restaurant, Bai Xiangning's attitude towards food made him realize for the first time that cooking was not a boring and repetitive task, but a way to constantly create delicious food that surprises customers.After the busy lunch time, the three people in the store had a moment of leisure. Bai Xiangning and Qiao Ping were wiping the table, while Fang Xin collected all the kitchen waste and planned to throw it into the garbage not far outside the door. in the car.Hey, Master Fang took out the trash, why hasn't he come back yetAfter Qiao Ping finished wiping the table, she found that Fang Xin was not there yet, so she said doubtfully.I'll go outside and have a look.Bai Xiangning walked to the garbage truck but found no sign of Fang Xin.Hey, aren't you here Bai Xiangning looked around, and then walked towards the back of the garbage truck. She seemed to hear a familiar voice just now, and Fang Xin should be nearby.She walked around a wall and saw Fang Xin's back to her. Bai Xiangning walked over quickly. Fang XinI won't go backBai Xiangning:Fang Xin said he would not go back, but he had only been to the restaurant for a few days.Bai Xiangning quickly reflected on whether it was because she, the boss, did not give enough care to her employees or that the salary she gave did not meet Fang Xin's expectations. When she paid out the salary, Fang Xin Ming Ming agreed readily.Could it be that he felt that there were too many customers in the small restaurant and it was too busyBai Xiangning was worried.It's hard to find a chef with good conditions in all aspects, but after only a few days, he gets upset and says he doesn't want to go back. What should I doFang Xin still had his back to her, and Bai Xiangning stood not far from him, racking her brains to think of how to stabilize Fang Xin so that he would continue to return to the small restaurant.You said someone saw me working as a waiter in a shabby roadside restaurant. Fang Xin snorted coldly, yes, he read it right, I am now the chef of the Bai Family Restaurant.Well, Fang Xin seems to be talking to someone elseBai Xiangning moved to the side, and suddenly realized what she was wearing when she saw what Fang Xin was wearing on her ears.It turned out that he was wearing a Bluetooth headset and talking to someone on the phone, so she couldn't blame her for not noticing it just now.Since she was on the phone, it meant that she was not talking to her just now, so she had better not listen to them.Just when she was about to turn around and leave, Fang Xin's angry voice came from behind.You said I was sorry for Wei Ding JiIsn't Wei Ding Ji a hotel chain that is well-known in Jinghua CityBai Xiangning couldn't help but stop.The person who called Fang Xin was the manager of the Weidingji branch. After Fang Xin left angrily that day, he thought that Fang Xin would come back after calming down for a few days. Unexpectedly, he later He directly asked someone to submit his resignation without even showing his face.After waiting for a few days, Fang Xin did not regret it. Instead, he heard another news, saying that he saw Fang Xin now working as a chef in a small restaurant.The store manager didn't believe it, so he called Fang Xin himself.After some earnest persuasion, Fang Xin remained indifferent and had no intention of returning to Wei Ding Ji. The store manager also became angry with embarrassment. If it weren't for the fact that Fang Xin was an old employee of Wei Ding Ji, he would never have put down his dignity and took the initiative to call Fang Xin. As a result, he called Fang Xin, but Fang Xin didn't appreciate it at all.The store manager got angry and said without hesitation: Fang Xin, don't forget who trained you, Wei Ding Ji. If it weren't for Wei Ding Ji, would you be able to have the ability you have now You are not grateful and have given up your job. Are you worthy of our Wei DingjiFang Xin found it incredible that I'm sorry the store manager of Wei Ding Ji said that during the two years I was at Wei Ding Ji, I was the first one to come to the store every day and the last one to leave. I have always worked diligently and never fought for anything. I did all the hard work that others were not willing to do. Everyone who came in with me got a salary increase, but I was the only one who still got the same money as two years ago. coolieAs Fang Xin spoke, he felt more and more angry. It's not that I didn't know that you were partial to Liu Wangfei. I just always had illusions about Wei Dingji and felt that I belonged there. But what you did later It's so chillingI don't know what was said over there, but Fang Xin's voice became louder. The development you are talking about is using mass-produced semi-finished dishes for guests to eat.After shouting this sentence, Fang Xin seemed to have exhausted all his strength, and his voice lowered, "That's it, I will not look back on Wei Ding Ji again, and Wei Ding Ji will be with me no matter what in the future." Nothing to do. Working together, I wish you better and better.The store manager cursed: You heartless white-eyed wolf, I'm beepingThe store manager's eyes widened and he looked at the phone that had been hung up. He said in disbelief: This Fang Xin actually dared to hang up on me.The other people in the kitchen were too nervous to breathe, for fear of offending the store manager.Since Chef Fang left, the store manager has become irritable. The store is in a very depressed and tense state every day, and even the mistake of serving the wrong dish to the customer has occurred twice in a row.The store manager nodded and bowed to apologize to the customers, then came to the kitchen and cursed them all, which made people panic and feel like they were walking on thin ice.At this time, the store manager's roaring voice spread throughout the entire kitchen.None of you are allowed to contact Fang Xin again. Once he leaves, you will never come back.Everyone in the kitchen thought, it seems like you are the only one who has contacted him so far.Many of them are from Liu Wangfei's side, so naturally they don't want Fang Xin, a competitor, to come back. No one under Fang Xin ever thought of contacting him. After all, they had worked hard to get the opportunity to work at Weidingji. How could they take risks for othersThe store manager's eyes moved around their faces, and he couldn't tell that the people underneath had their own thoughts.He said sternly: You must know that it is a great honor for you to stay at Wei Ding Ji.

Work hard for me and never relax for a moment.Until Fang Xin hung up the phone and turned around to walk this way, Bai Xiangning was still in extreme shock.She had always thought that Fang Xin came from some small restaurant, but she never expected that his former owner was Wei Ding Ji.Boss BaiFang Xin's voice brought Bai Xiangning back from her thoughts. She realized that it was inappropriate for her to appear here at this moment, but she did not hide it too much, but said frankly: I had originally planned to I didn't mean to call you backIt's okay, it's okay to hear it.Bai Xiangning paused and then asked: Were you a chef at Weidingji beforeThe reputation of Wei Dingji in Jinghua City is so great that no one knows about it. Bai Xiangning has also been admiring its name for a long time, but after hearing what Fang Xin said just now, it seems that It was different from the Wei Ding Ji she imagined.Yes, I did it for a while.Bai Xiangning felt a little uncomfortable when she thought about the salary she paid to Fang Xin. Could it be that the salary she paid to Fang Xin was too little Fang Xin used to be in Weidingji, and his salary must be much higher than this, but now in If her salary suddenly drops, will there be a big gap in his heartSo she weighed her tone and asked: Well, your remuneration at Wei Dingji must have been very high at that time, rightFang Xin realized what Bai Xiangning was worried about, and Fang Xin was actually afraid that she would think that he was a Buddha that she could not afford to pay homage to, and that she would not want him to continue working in the small restaurant.Fang Xin coughed and his expression immediately dropped. He lowered his voice and said: Hey, it's not high, just 5,000.5000. Is that the salary of your chefFang Xin continued to sigh. In fact, my salary is considered high. Some cooks only get 3,000. Fang Xin said while peeking at Bai Xiangning's reaction.Bai Xiangning took a breath. She really didn't expect that a hotel chain as big as Wei Dingji would be so stingy towards its employees. She, an outsider, couldn't stand it. No wonder Fang Xin, as an employee, wanted to run away. She would run if the road changed for her.Bai Xiangning, who was originally worried that her salary was not high enough, looked at Fang Xin with a very loving expression, then patted him on the shoulder and said firmly: Don't worry, I won't treat you badly when you work here. When small restaurants develop in the future, wages will continue to rise, come onFang Xin breathed a sigh of relief.It seems that Boss Bai has completely believed what he said. Since he has talked about his long-term development in the small restaurant, he will definitely not be allowed to pack up and leave for the time being.He just said that his salary at Wei Ding Ji is only 5,000. In fact, adding an extra 0 at the end is his real salary.And when he left Wei Ding Ji, it was not because Bai Xiangning thought that the salary was too low, but because he felt that Wei Ding Ji was no longer the place he originally longed for.He is not a particularly talented chef, and his cooking skills have reached the current level only because he has to work harder than others. He has a rigid mind and will keep moving forward without looking back if he sees a reason.Wei Ding Ji's current philosophy ran counter to him, so he chose to leave.It had only been a few days since he joined the small restaurant, but he felt that he had made an extremely right decision.At the beginning, the store manager told him that the use of semi-finished products was a general trend in the entire catering industry. He was shaken in his belief at that time. He couldn't help asking himself whether it was really what the store manager said. , all hotels will do thisBut that night, he walked into Bai's small restaurant, and then he suddenly realized that no, not all restaurants would make the same choice. There are always some people who insist on their own choices. Heart.Bai Xiangning helped him regain his long-lost love for food and found the meaning of continuing to persevere in this industry.Of course, love cannot be used as a meal. Fang Xin chose the Bai Family Restaurant because he felt that the restaurant had unlimited potential for development. Here, he would definitely be able to have ten times and a hundred times more money than at Wei Ding Ji. harvest.

Chapter 29DingHao Yu took out the lunch box from the microwave and walked to his work station.In addition to Hao Yu, many people in the company choose to bring their own meals, but Hao Yu found that there have been significantly fewer people bringing meals recently.There are only two microwave ovens in the company break room. In the past, just waiting for the microwave oven would take ten or twenty minutes, but these two days she didn't even have to wait, and she could heat up the meal directly.She has insisted on bringing meals for a long time. From the beginning, she was excited and wanted to cook one thing a day, but now she feels painful when she thinks about having to cook after work, and what to eat every day has become a problem for her. a big problem.After sitting at her workstation, she opened her lunch box and prepared to eat. After taking two bites, she suddenly smelled a particularly fragrant smell.Hao Yu raised her head and looked around to see which colleague brought such delicious food. After looking around, she found that the smell seemed to come from Zhou Fei opposite.In her impression, Zhou Fei was a big takeout seller and had never brought his own food.Zhou Fei was concentrating on eating hard, so Hao Yu quickly stood up and took a look while he was not paying attention. He was holding a packing box in his hand.It seems to be another takeaway.Hao Yu lost interest. Although she felt that cooking was a bit troublesome, she still chose to cook by herself rather than eating unhealthy takeout. Not to mention whether it was delicious or not, at least it was hygienic and safe.So she continued to eat, but she didn't know what was going on. The ribs that tasted delicious last night now had no taste at all. The aroma of the ribs was completely covered up by the takeout Zhou Fei ordered, lingering around. It's all the smell of his takeaway food.Hao Yu slowly stuffed a piece of spareribs into his mouth, which tasted like chewing wax.While Zhou Fei was eating, he was talking to the people next to him: "The rice bowl in the small restaurant is so delicious. Even if I eat it for ten or twenty days in a row, I won't get tired of it."His colleague also echoed, "How many people have been saved by opening the small restaurant at noon Finally, we no longer need to be tortured by takeaway food."Judging from what he meant, couldn't it be that what they ordered for lunch today wasn't takeoutHao Yu could no longer suppress his inner curiosity and asked them: "Where did you buy your lunch I see that you ate very deliciously."Not only was it fragrant, it was simply fragrant. Smelling the aroma of their rice, Hao Yu couldn't eat the food in his lunch box at all.Zhou Fei had almost finished eating. When he heard Hao Yu ask him, he immediately took the initiative to help Hao Yu secure Baijia's small restaurant.He praised the small restaurant so much that Hao Yu was stunned for a moment, wondering if this small restaurant was so delicious. It sounded like an ordinary small restaurant. Could Zhou Fei be eating out Selling it for too long, a little delicious food can make him fussBut the smell he just smelled was too fragrant, so Hao Yu made up his mind to weed the grass on the weekend. After eating it, he would definitely not miss it anymore.It's eleven o'clock on Saturday morning, inside the Bai family restaurant.What do you want to eatQiao Ping stood in front of the ordering counter and asked about the lady with the little girl in front of her.After listening to Zhou Fei's strong recommendation a few days ago, Hao Yu took his daughter over to try this Bai family restaurant on the weekend. Zhou Fei had teriyaki chicken drumstick rice bowl that day, and Hao Yu also planned to order this.Just when she was taking an order, her daughter standing next to her suddenly said:Mom, I want to drink that lychee ice jasmineHao Yu followed her gaze and found that her daughter was talking about the ice drinks placed on the counter, which was placed by Qiao Pingcai.Due to the addition of ice cubes, some small water droplets appeared on the outer wall of the transparent glass, and the color of the ice drink looked good.However, Hao Yu still doesn't plan to give this to his daughter. Cold drinks sold outside already contain a lot of additives, and the ones made in restaurants are even more insecure. Placing them on a conspicuous counter must be attractive. Just a gimmick for customers.Hao Yu knelt down and whispered to her daughter: "We don't drink this. Mommy will go back and cook you some rock sugar pear. It's also delicious. It's much healthier than this. I don't know how much saccharin is added to this drink. It tastes right." Poor health.She lowered her voice, but what she just said was still heard by a customer behind her. That person was an old customer of Bai Family Restaurant and a die-hard fan.Madam, have you ever drank the lychee iced jasmine from Bai's Little RestaurantHis tone was a bit harsh, so Hao Yu frowned and said displeased: Of course I haven't drank.You've never tasted it, so why are you saying that the drinks sold by others are unhealthy Aren't you talking nonsenseIThe commotion here quickly attracted the attention of the following guests. They listened in general and understood the ins and outs of the matter, and started talking one after another.I can guarantee that the iced drinks sold in Baijia Little Restaurant are not inferior to those of specialized milk tea shops, and are even much better than those shops.Yes, yes, I used to love drinking milk tea, but since I drank the lychee iced jasmine from the small restaurant, I order a cup every day and will never go to other milk tea shops again.Another elderly grandmother said: At first, I had the same idea as you. I felt that this kind of drink was not healthy and should not be given to children. But one time, my grandson secretly bought a cup and let me take a sip. , the taste is so refreshing, refreshing and delicious that even I, an old woman, can't help but fall in love with it. Since then, I don't need to tell my grandson that I will often come here to buy it for him.Hao Yu didn't expect that her unintentional words would be denounced by so many people. She stood there, a little embarrassed.But when I think about it carefully, what she just said is really untenable. She has never drank this lychee ice jasmine. How can she categorically tell her daughter that this drink must be unhealthyA girl helped her out. She said to Hao Yu: The ice drinks sold here are really different from other places. They are made with real ingredients and no additives. You can buy a cup and try it first. If you think it's okay Give your daughter another drink.Well, that's a good thing. The other customers are not so entangled. Hao Yu breathed a sigh of relief and said to Qiao Ping: Give me a glass of lychee iced jasmine and two teriyaki chicken legs and rice.Qiao Ping heard the arguments just made by the customers, but as an employee of a small restaurant, she felt that it was better not to get too involved and let the customers solve the problem themselves.What's more, this is not a big deal. What Hao Yu said at the beginning was very normal. As caterers, they will face more or less doubts from customers. If they concentrate on making good food, customers' concerns will naturally be eliminated.Hao Yu and her daughter sat down on their seats and looked at the beautiful ice drink in front of her mother. Her daughter was ready to take a sip. Can I take a sipno. Hao Yu picked up the cup and decided to taste it himself first.There were some ice cubes in the cup, and she shook it slightly. The ice cubes collided in the drink, making a pleasant sound, and a faint scent of lychee floated in the air.Hao Yu took a sip.The highly sweet lychees are mixed with the elegant jasmine tea. The two blend perfectly, but retain the characteristics of each other. They swirled in Hao Yu's mouth, and were finally swallowed and slid into his throat.There was still a lot of white pulp at the bottom, so Hao Yu picked up the straw, stirred it, and sucked up a few plump lychee pulps.There is a thin layer of drink wrapped around the pulp, but the drink on the outside is absorbed by the mouth as soon as you take it into your mouth, so you can enjoy the original sweet aroma of the lychee.I have to say that Hao Yu was stunned after just taking a sip. As she chewed the sweet pulp, the surprise in her eyes became even more obvious.Dear good mother, just give me a sip, just a sip.Hao Yu was so intoxicated that he didn't hear his daughter speak at all.The daughter sitting opposite her was on pins and needles. Looking at her mother, she knew that the drink was delicious. She was anxious and wanted to grab the cup in Hao Yu's hand.As a result, Hao Yu turned the cup in his hand without hesitation and placed it out of his daughter's reach.Her daughter: The most wonderful mother is you.Hao Yu quickly drank a whole glass of drink without realizing it. She felt that her whole body had become ice-cold and so comfortable that she was almost floating.Mother.Her daughter's voice brought her back to reality. When she turned her head, she saw her daughter staring at her with an extremely resentful look.An empty cup in hand.Oops, I accidentally drank too much and didn't give my daughter a sip. All of it went into her own stomach.AhemHao Yu coughed twice to cover up, and then said to her daughter: I'm sorry, honey, mom just wanted to give you a taste, but she accidentally finished the drink. Mom will buy you another drink now. You Sit here and wait for me.Please bring me another glass of lychee iced jasmine, with less ice.This cup is for his daughter, so Hao Yu specially asked Qiao Ping to put less ice cubes, otherwise even if the ingredients are very healthy, her daughter will easily have diarrhea after drinking it.By the time she returned to her seat with her second glass of lychee iced jasmine, the two rice bowls they had just ordered were ready.At this moment, a strong and attractive aroma is exuding.The daughter was still angry that she didn't give her a sip of the drink just now, and now she was in a mood. As soon as the rice bowl was served, she started eating by herself without waiting for Hao Yu to come over.After she took two bites, her unhappiness about not having an ice drink disappeared immediately. Now her whole body was firmly occupied by the delicious taste of teriyaki chicken drumsticks in her mouth, and she had no time to think about anything else.delicious.Hao Yu sat down. The teriyaki chicken leg rice bowl in front of her was more attractive than what she had seen at Zhou Fei's place two days ago. The chicken leg meat that had just been cooked was cut into long strips and wrapped in a rich and shiny sauce. The juice is neatly placed on the rice with distinct grains.Mom, you should eat quickly, this chicken leg meat is really delicious. My daughter's cheeks were bulging from eating, and she said to her vaguely.Seeing how delicious her daughter was eating, how could Hao Yu still be able to endure itShe picked up the spoon, quickly took a big spoonful of meat and rice and put it into her mouth.This chicken thigh, this sauce, and this rice, everything struck her taste buds, making her eat one bite after another uncontrollably.

Chapter 30At noon on Monday, the sun was blazing outside. Zhou Fei and his colleagues walked out of the office building under the scorching sun. In order to get ahead of everyone, they started racing again. But even so, after arriving at Bai's small restaurant , there are still many people queuing inside.But fortunately, you can turn on the air conditioner after entering the store. It's not like being outside and burning your whole body.When Zhou Fei arrived in line, he said to Qiao Ping: I want a teriyaki chicken drumstick rice bowl, please pack it.After scanning the QR code to pay, he stood aside and waited for his colleagues to finish their orders.He looked around the store and saw that there were a lot of people at noon recently, so he always packed up food and brought it to the company to eat, watching the football game while eating, so that people could get short-term happiness.When Hao Yu arrived at the small restaurant, Zhou Fei and the others were preparing to go out with their packed bags.Sister Hao Yu, Zhou Fei was surprised. He never thought that he could meet Hao Yu in a small restaurant. Hao Yu always brought dinner to the party at noon.You've all finished shopping. Hao Yu saw the bag in his hand and said with a smile.Yes, Sister Hao Yu, why are you hereHao Yu said: You recommended this place to me that day. I brought my daughter here on the weekend. I ordered lychee, iced jasmine and teriyaki chicken drumstick rice bowl. I was instantly conquered. So, I thought at noon today. Then continue to come over and order one to take home.Thinking of the way he and his daughter got carried away eating that day, Hao Yu was a little embarrassed. Fortunately, no acquaintances saw it that day.Sister Hao Yu, let's go back first. The lunch break at noon was not long, and Zhou Fei still had a lot of dinner videos waiting to be watched when he went back.Hao Yu said: Well, you guys go back first.At the same time, a colleague in the company passed by Zhou Fei's workstation and said with some surprise: Why can't I see Zhou Fei at twelve o'clock latelySomeone familiar with the matter said casually: He went down to buy food.Ah, for being so diligent, didn't he always order takeout beforeJust at this time Zhou Fei came back, and the colleague who had just spoken jumped to his side and said curiously: Let me see what you bought.Zhou Fei thought to himself, another person is about to fall into the trap.He sat down on his seat and then opened the lid of the box.No need for him to say anything more, the strong aroma of teriyaki chicken legs has already captured his colleagues. The colleague held the bowl and said pitifully:Damn it, give me a piece-When it was about to close in the evening, Fang Xin said to Bai Xiangning: Boss Bai, a very large seafood market has been opened nearby. I went shopping that day and there are all kinds of seafood in it. If you call If you want to buy seafood, you can go there to have a look. There are many varieties and the price is cheap.seafoodAlthough the wet market she often goes to is very large, there are very few seafood sellers and very few varieties, so the small restaurant has never served seafood dishes.When Fang Xin said that a new seafood market had opened nearby, Bai Xiangning immediately became interested. She said: OK, then you can send me the location of the seafood market and I will go and have a look tomorrow morning.Fang Xin sent her the location and Bai Xiangning collected it, preparing to get up early tomorrow.At about seven o'clock the next day, Bai Xiangning found the seafood market according to the position given to her by Fang Xin. The market's signboard was very large, with several large red characters hanging high, which looked very conspicuous.Outside the market were some retail investors selling small fish and shrimps. Bai Xiangning did not stop, but walked directly inside.The first shop near the door sells king crabs. It occupies the best position and the business is good. There are two or three customers gathered around, all picking crabs.Compared with ordinary crabs, the king crab is huge in size and has very long claws. It clings to the glass with its claws and fangs, as if it is about to break free from the glass box in the next second. It looks very fierce.However, Bai Xiangning didn't plan to buy this kind of large seafood, so she just looked at it briefly and continued walking forward.After passing several businesses, she stopped in front of a shop that sold all kinds of small seafood. There were several water tanks on the ground, including razor clams, clams, and crayfish. It looks fresh and lively.Girl, what do you want to buyShe pointed to one of the water tanks and said: Boss, how do you sell razor clams20 a pound, the market has just opened recently, the more you buy, the more discounts you will get, girls, it's up to you how much you want.Bai Xiangning squatted down. The razor clam in the water tank was big. Its two plump tentacles stretched out and retracted. It breathed deeply and shallowly in the water. The flesh looked very plump.She looked at the crayfish placed next to them again, and they were all alive and kicking. The claws, which were huge compared to their bodies, danced majestically in the air, as if they were provoking Bai Xiangning.Bai Xiangning thought to herself, if you look again, I will eat you.She stood up, boss, how much are clams and crayfish per poundClams are 8 yuan and crayfish are 10 yuan.So how much should I buy to get the discountThe wholesale price is only available if you buy more than 10 kilograms of each variety, and each kilogram is 2 yuan lower than the price I just quoted you.Bai Xiangning came today just to explore and couldn't buy so much, so she said to the boss: Boss, please add a

WeChat account first. If I need it later, can you deliver it to my door I'm a bit far away from here. Buy it. There are so many that it is inconvenient to take them back.The boss's eyes lit up and he thought that this was a potential big customer. She couldn't ignore him, so he said enthusiastically: Okay, okay, I'll add you.After adding it, Bai Xiangning said: Today I will buy some and try it out. If it tastes good, I will contact you via WeChat to purchase it.She looked at several water tanks on the ground, and then said to the boss: "Let's get one pound each of razor clams and crayfish."okayFor the purpose of subsequent business, the boss specially picked the good ones for her and put them in the bag. Bai Xiangning could see clearly and knew what the boss was thinking. She smiled and said nothing.After buying these, Bai Xiangning looked at the time. It was not yet eight o'clock, so she walked around the market again. When she returned to the store, it was just over eight o'clock.Qiao Ping looked at the several bags she was carrying and stepped forward to take them. Hey, Boss Bai, all you bought are seafood.Fang Xin also came over, opened the bag and took a look. For a moment, he didn't expect what Bai Xiangning planned to cook.Bai Xiangning said with a smile: The weather is getting hot, so I plan to make a small seafood dish with sauce to cool down the customers.

Chapter 31Braised seafood is a cold dish, just right for

the hot weather.Fang Xin and Qiao Ping poured the clams and razor clams bought by Bai Xiangning into the pool, and then started to drain the water so that all the seafood was soaked in the clean water. This was a purification process that allowed the clams and razor clams to slowly When the sand in the body is spit out, the teeth will not bite the sand suddenly and affect the taste when eating.Soak for about an hour. After the sand is basically spit out, use a soft-bristled toothbrush to brush off the dirt on the outer shell. This completes the basic pretreatment.Bai Xiangning was preparing seasonings on the side, which is the most important sauce for small seafood.In order to make the aroma of the sauce stronger, you first need to fry the oil. Pour an appropriate amount of peanut oil into the pot, then pour in all the onions, ginger, coriander and bay leaves at once, and turn on low heat to absorb the aroma of the ingredients. Slowly push them out, and when the edges of the spices turn brown, you can use a slotted spoon to take out all the fried spices.Bai Xiangning put finely chopped garlic, salt, a little chili powder and white sesame seeds in the bowl in advance. When the oil was heated, the aroma that had been sleeping in these condiments suddenly burst out, Bai Xiangning. Ning was so close that he felt the strong aroma most directly.She took a small spoon from the side, stirred the seasonings in the bowl, and then added the remaining seasonings. Needless to say, light soy sauce, dark soy sauce, oyster sauce, and fish sauce must be added. There are also the two most important seasonings, vinegar and sugar. Vinegar is used to enhance the flavor, while sugar is used to enhance the freshness. Only a small amount of these two seasonings can greatly increase the flavor of the finished product. Without either, the flavor will be poor. No soul.Finally, you need to add water, so that the juice is ready.At the same time, Fang Xin and Qiao Ping poured the washed seafood into a large pot, added a large pot full of water, added some ginger slices to remove the fishy smell, and then began to blanch the water.After the seafood is cooked, it needs to be quickly put into water with ice cubes. This can not only cool down quickly, but more importantly, it can make the meat of the seafood firm and elastic, and maintain the taste to the greatest extent.After half an hour, the heat of the seafood had dissipated. Bai Xiangning poured the juice on the seafood and added a few slices of lemon with seeds removed.Qiao Ping said impatiently: Boss Bai, is this ready to eatNo. Bai Xiangning sealed the large bowl of seafood with plastic wrap, and then put the bowl in the refrigerator. It will taste better if it is refrigerated for two hours.The seafood Bai Xiangning bought was just enough for the three of them to eat. She was just testing the dishes first this time, not only to test the quality of the seafood, but also to test the preparation of the sauce. Waiting for the three of them. I have tasted all of them and will only officially introduce this new product if I think it is acceptable.After the busy lunch rush hour, the small seafood in sauce refrigerated in the refrigerator was almost ready. Bai Xiangning took out the bowl, opened the plastic wrap, and sprinkled a handful of coriander into it.At this time, the last customer in the store just walked out, so Bai Xiangning turned around and said to the other two people: The small seafood in laozhi is ready, go and try it.Then she walked to the door and was about to close it when she suddenly felt a resistance on her hand.Well, is the door stuck with somethingShe took a closer look and saw that there was actually a hand against the door. Then, the owner of the hand put his head in through the door. It was the last guest who had just left.Bai Xiangning was confused: Did this customer leave something in the storeShe let go of her hand to close the door, and the customers outside the door took advantage of the situation and entered the store again.He said with expectation: Boss Bai, when I went out just now, I seemed to hear you telling me to eat some small seafood. I don't know if I heard it wrong.Bai Xiangning: It's true that you heard wrong. She was clearly calling Fang Xin and Qiao Ping just now, but she was accidentally overheard by the guests.The customer obviously didn't give up and took two more steps into the store, just in time to see the small seafood in sauce that Bai Xiangning had just taken out from the refrigerator, even with the plastic wrap torn off.As a cold dish, the flavor of the small seafood in the sauce is not very strong, but the sour and spicy taste still lingers in the whole store, making it impossible to ignore.The seafood is soaked in the fish juice, and there are dots of coriander and lemon slices scattered on the surface, making it mouth-watering.The customer took a sip of saliva, and then looked at Bai Xiangning longingly, "Wow, Boss Bai, I saw it all. That bowl is filled with the small seafood you mentioned, right"Bai Xiangning followed his gaze and turned around. Oh no, she was caught by a customer.That one was actually our lunch because the Lao Zhi Seafood had not been officially launched, so Bai Xiangning did not tell customers that this was a new product that the store planned to release.The customer obviously ate a lot at noon, but at this moment he felt that his stomach was protesting again, so he pitifully said to Bai Xiangning: Boss Bai, just let me have a taste. , just have a small tasteBai Xiangning was still hesitating. It's not that she couldn't bear to eat this bite, it's just that it was her first time to make small seafood in sauce, and she hadn't even tasted it yet. The recipe of the seasoning may need to be improved. If it is given to customers rashly, if the customers are not satisfied, then Trouble.Woo hoo, Boss Bai, I'm really starving to death. I'm so hungry, so hungry, so hungry. I'm so hungry that I can't stand it anymore.Bai Xiangning:If you hadn't just eaten two large plates of rice bowls at my restaurant, then your words might still be somewhat convincing.But Bai Xiangning really couldn't bear his look like an abandoned dog, so she could only agree, okay.The customer raised his hand and swore, Boss Bai, don't worry, I will never tell anyone that you turned on the small stove for me after I finished eating.Bai Xiangning thought to herself, it's okay if you don't say this. Once you say it, I think you will definitely tell others.Qiao Ping handed the customer a pair of clean chopsticks, and he immediately smiled.Four people sat at a table, and the customer was the one eating. He wanted to be more reserved at first, but when he saw the small seafood in the sauce, all his rationality disappeared. There was only one thought left in his mind, and that was to hurry up and get the small seafood. eatThere were three kinds of seafood in the bowl. He didn't choose specifically, but ate whatever he picked up. The first thing that fell into his chopsticks was the clam that had opened its shell. The shell and the meat inside were all. After being coated in the clam juice, he flicked it, and the clam meat came out of its shell and was stuffed into his mouth.The first thing that came into contact with the tip of his tongue was the fresh, sour and slightly spicy clam juice, which tasted like a light lemon aroma. When his teeth bit into it, the naturally delicious taste of the clam meat came out, but he hadn't yet. Feel it more, and the small clam meat is swallowed, which is not satisfying at all.So this time he specially picked up a slightly larger razor clam. The eating process was the same as before, but the meat of razor clams was obviously thicker than clams. It was plump and tender when chewed in his mouth. The addition of the juice seemed to make his mouth reverberate. While listening to the symphony, all kinds of flavors are colliding fiercely, like layers of waves constantly lapping the mouth.The sauce prepared by Bai Xiangning is not strong in taste and does not cover up the taste of the seafood itself at all. Instead, it makes it even more delicious, making it almost impossible to stop eating.The clams and razor clams were processed very cleanly, with no sediment at all. Unlike the rice noodles he used to eat outside, he had to spit out several mouthfuls of sand after eating one mouthful of rice noodles. Once, his teeth were even scratched. The sand collapsed a bit, and the experience was as bad as it could be. Now, he doesn't even dare to eat this kind of seafood outside.But the small seafood I ate this time was completely different. There was no sand, and the meat was very tender. After several hours of refrigeration, the flavor of the juice penetrated into the seafood better. In the small meat, It combines extremely complex aromas, fresh, sweet, spicy, sour, all kinds of flavors intertwined together, leaving people with endless aftertaste.Obviously there is only a small amount of meat, but the residual fragrance can stay in your mouth for a long time after eating.The customer was intoxicated with the meal. When he came back to his senses, there were many shells piled in front of him. He looked at the other people who had clearly fewer shells than him, and he felt uncomfortable afterwards. Good intentions come up.Ahhhh, Boss Bai, will you think that he is so thick-skinned Not only did he come here to eat, but he actually ate so muchHe tried hard to save his image in front of Bai Xiangning, so he said: Boss Bai, is there still a shortage of people in your store Can I apply for a job I can do whatever you want. I can mop the floor, wipe the table, and take out the trash. Can do it allBai Xiangning just said that this small seafood with sauce is their lunch. He thought to himself that even lunch in the small restaurant is so delicious, so if he works here, wouldn't he be able to eat such delicious food every dayI'm so excited just thinking about it. I can't wait to work in a small restaurant tomorrow.After hearing his words, Qiao Ping's back stiffened, and she looked at the customer as if facing an enemy. She was a little anxious, why was this person like this It wasn't enough for him to eat small seafood, but he also came to the store to steal her job.Fortunately, Bai Xiangning explained in time: This is actually not our lunch, but a new product planned by the store. Today is the trial stage. We originally wanted to try it first and then see if there is any need to improve the taste. of.The customer immediately said: Boss Bai, you are too humble. There is absolutely nothing that needs to be improved about this little seafood. The taste is definitely the best. I can guarantee you that this dish will be sold out as soon as it is served.Thinking of the fierce competition for food when the small restaurant released new products in the past, he added another sentence: Boss Bai, tell me when the small seafood in the sauce will be officially launched.When the time comes, he will come over in advance and stay there. If he can be the first one, he will definitely not be the second person to grab the new product.Bai Xiangning said hesitantly: I haven't thought about it yet, but in the next two days, when I decide to officially launch the new version, I will make an announcement in the group.The good customer didn't ask any more questions. He had already pinned the small restaurant's customer base. As long as Bai Xiangning made an announcement, he would definitely see it immediately.

Chapter 32After having a free meal of seafood in a small restaurant, Meng Jun was in an extremely happy mood for the next whole day.He wanted to tell everyone around him that he had tasted a new product that was not yet available in the small restaurant, but he kept in mind the promise he made in front of Bai Xiangning and said that he would never tell anyone else about it.Boss Bai has already said that this is a new product that has not been officially launched yet, and there may be some improvements that need to be made. If he says it out loud, wouldn't it affect the restaurant's businessHe can't eat other people's seafood for nothing and not keep his word.How can I be worthy of Boss Bai like thatHow could he deserve the super delicious seafood he put into his stomachSo after he got through the initial excitement, he fell into extreme confusion.He wanted to grab everyone who passed by him and talk about this thing that he was proud of.But he couldn't speak, he was almost suffocated.If he had known that eating Laozhi seafood would put him in such a dilemma, he would have definitelyNo.Meng Jun forcibly cut off the thoughts in his mind. He did not regret that he pushed open the door of the small restaurant and shamelessly touched the small seafood.If you give him another chance to start over, he will definitely be thicker-skinned and eat more.Meng Jun, what are you thinking about Your mouth is grinning to the back of your head.The colleague sitting next to him saw that his expression was unpredictable all morning, sometimes confused, sometimes excited, and sometimes dejected, so he asked him what was going on.As if something had struck his mind, Meng Jun quickly calmed down all his expressions and said dryly: It's nothing, everything is normal.Colleague: I see that everything is not normal with you.Meng Jun is still savoring the sweet and sour taste of the small seafood in the sauce. The tender and smooth taste of clams still seems to be left on the inner wall of his mouth, so he can no longer maintain his expression as he holds it, with a crazy smile on his face. road:I really want to eat it againMy colleague wondered: What do you want to eatAhem, nothing.The colleague lost interest and continued to work on his own work while turning his chair.

Why don't you continue asking meIf you ask me again, maybe I'll tell you.But his colleague didn't give him another look, but focused on staring at the computer screen.Meng Jun was so anxious that he could not wait to rip his heart out at his colleagues in the next second.He could no longer suppress his desire to show off, so he pretended to be casual and approached his colleague, and then coughed.The colleague stared at him with a look that said something was wrong with him. Meng Jun selectively ignored his gaze and asked directly:Do you like seafoodMy colleague's eyes lit up and his head suddenly started to spin. I love it so much.His hometown is a coastal city. When he was a child, the most common thing on the dining table at home was all kinds of seafood. Basically, they were all freshly caught that day. Not to mention they tasted very exciting.Meng Jun also said excitedly: I just ate some very delicious small seafood in laozhi yesterday.Small seafood in sauce, my colleague thought thoughtfully, you ate it near hereMeng Jun nodded fiercely, yes, yes.When making small seafood dishes, the most important thing is to pay attention to the original taste of the ingredients, and the freshness of the seafood is very high. If there is any staleness, the whole dish will taste lifeless and tasteless.The colleague leaned back on his chair. Jinghua City is an inland city and there is not much seafood. Moreover, he has eaten at almost all the seafood restaurants nearby, and none of them can satisfy his taste. I guess Meng Jun was talking about one of them.If it were a store nearby, the small seafood in Lao Zhi mentioned by Meng Jun wouldn't be that delicious. After all, the seafood in nearby stores isn't very fresh.Meng Jun clearly saw the excitement on his colleague's face fade away, and then returned to the uninterested look before.He wondered if his colleagues didn't like the practice of fishing for juice.He whispered in a low voice: Since you don't like to eat, then when the small restaurant officially opens a new one, I will go and eat by myself.My colleague's ears twitched. You just said a small restaurant.Meng Jun remained silent.Could it be that the small seafood you mentioned is a new dish served in small restaurantsThe colleague immediately lowered his head and opened WeChat, but he did not see any new announcement in the small restaurant group. The last announcement was the last one.Seeing Meng Jun's face full of merit and fame, his colleagues guessed that he was selling out, so he strangled Meng Jun's neck and threatened him: Tell him quickly, I won't let him go until you tell him.Hmm, after two days, wouldn't you know that Meng Jun was choked and couldn't say a complete sentence, but he felt so proud, haha, he was the only one in the world. People, I ate ahead of time the new Laozhi small seafood dish that the small restaurant will soon launch.Who else has this honor besides himAfter the customers left that day, the three people in the small restaurant got rid of all the remaining small seafood. Then Bai Xiangning asked Qiao Ping and Fang Xin,Do you think there is anything that needs improvementQiao Ping has always boasted about Bai Xiangning's cooking skills. No matter what she cooks, Qiao Ping will always say it's delicious, and she actually thinks so. Bai Xiangning mainly wanted to hear if Fang Xin had any opinions.But since Fang Xin came to the small restaurant, he was completely captured by Bai Xiangning's craftsmanship and became her number two fan.Fang Xin shook his head and said sincerely: Boss Bai, I think the small seafood you made is quite delicious. If you put it out at this level, you can definitely capture the stomachs of all customers.He thought for a while and then added rigorously, of course, except for those who don't like seafood or are allergic to seafood.Although both Qiao Ping and Fang Xin agreed, Bai Xiangning still felt that there was room for improvement in this dish. She thought it was okay in terms of taste, but the texture of the seafood could be better.The day when Lao Zhi Seafood was officially launched was the hottest day since the beginning of summer in Jinghua City. Most people were indoors with air conditioners blowing on and could not feel the heat, but as soon as they went out, they would be hit by the blazing heat. The sun burns away one's appetite. Even if the sun goes down, the air is still scorching, which seriously affects people's appetite.In this weather, I really can't eat hot dishes, and my stomach is clamoring for some cool food to cool down.At ten o'clock in the morning, all the customers who were paying attention to the group news of the small restaurant saw a group announcement that suddenly popped up at the same time.Dear customers, the small restaurant has new Lao Zhi seafood, limited to 20 copies today, while supplies last.Words cannot shock the senses. Most people were just a little excited when they saw this group announcement, but when they saw Bai Xiangning's next post about small seafood in sauce, When the picture was taken, the group became excitedDamn it, what are you thinking about One second I was wondering when the restaurant would serve cold dishes, but the next second the boss announced a new one. Am I the prophet of the new centuryUpstairs, what you did was an afterthought at best. Woohoo, but this little seafood with juice looks so delicious, but it's limited to 20 portions. I feel like I can't get it at my speed.It doesn't matter, you're welcome to let us fast guys taste it for you.Wow, this little seafood really looks so fresh. You can already imagine how delicious it is. I really want to eat it today, but I have been so busy recently that I can only order takeout. Cried so muchEvery time there is a new release, the group will chatter about it for a long time. Bai Xiangning only watched it for two minutes, and then got into the busy work of preparing lunch.At noon, the first sentence after the first customer walked into the store wasBoss Bai, please bring me a small seafood dish to take away.He could have eaten in the store, but he chose to take it away and finally got the first one. He had to bring this hard-earned delicious food to the office.Let his colleagues watch him eat, and he will starve them to deathYour little seafood in sauce. Qiao Ping handed the packing bag to the customer, please take it.After the customer took it, he touched the bottom of the packaging box with his hand. It was ice cold and felt very comfortable.So he kept carrying the bag with his right hand and holding the bag with his left hand all the way back to the office.Then he opened the lid carelessly in the officeWhat does this taste likeAs soon as he opened the lid, his colleagues immediately formed a circle around him, all focusing on the round packing box on his desk.He said proudly: This is the small seafood I just bought in a small restaurant.colleagues:They quickly opened WeChat, and sure enough they saw a new announcement from the small restaurant. They just didn't check the group all morning, so they missed such important news.They were still regretting it. The person who bought the small seafood had already picked up his chopsticks and was about to eat it. His colleagues suddenly concentrated their fire on him alone.You saw the news and you didn't tell usO conscience of heaven and earth, I absolutely told you, but none of you paid attention to me at that time.The colleagues thought about it for a moment, and they seemed to have vaguely heard someone mentioning a small restaurant around ten o'clock, but they didn't pay attention at the time.Now, the only person in the office who bought the small seafood in juice was stuffing a big, fat razor clam into his mouth while others looked at him with envy and hatred.Hmm~This taste is too wonderful, rightEspecially when no one else can eat it and only he can eat it, the beauty increases exponentially.The colleagues around him could clearly hear the sound of him cracking the shell, and his intoxicated expression made people angry.So, the next second.Ahhhhh, don't grab my prawns, they are the ones I want to save for last.That piece of clam meat that fell out is also mine.The man who originally wanted to eat alone finally let out a roar under the attack of everyone.Little octopus, let me keep the little octopus. This is my final bottom line.

Chapter 33Oh, has it been sold outThe customer who spoke had a disappointed look on her face. She had come here specially to buy small seafood in the bright sun. At noon, even if she used a parasol, she could not completely block the heat wave coming from above her head. As soon as I entered the store, I learned the sad news that it was sold out.I'm really sorry. There's not a lot of small seafood available today. The supply will be increased in the future. Let's see if there's anything else you want to eat today.Bai Xiangning explained to the guest with an apologetic look.The customer knew that Bai's Little Restaurant would not prepare too much on the same day every time something new came out. She could only blame herself for coming too late and not grabbing the others, so she ordered one. Pair the rice bowl with a cold drink, and then sit in your seat and think fiercely, next time, I will definitely grab it next timeThe 20 servings of seafood on the first day were almost sold out within half an hour of the announcement. In order to avoid other customers making a wasted trip, Bai Xiangning could only hang up in the group again. An announcement.Today's portion of Laozhi seafood has been sold out, you can come back tomorrowAlthough she made the announcement in time, new customers were still pouring into the store at this time, all asking if the seafood was still available. Qiao Ping stood behind the counter and explained to them over and over again.Fortunately, the guests at Bai's small restaurant have always been very reasonable. Although they didn't feel heartbroken after eating the seafood, they still forced a smile and said to Bai Xiangning:Boss Bai, you must be more prepared tomorrow.Yes, why are the new ones so small every time They are gone in the blink of an eye. How can we, who are so far away, grab themBai Xiangning really underestimated customers' love for small seafood in Laozhi. Jinghua City is an inland city, and people rarely eat seafood. Before she launched the new product, she thought that 20 servings would be enough to sell for a day, but she didn't. I didn't expect it to sell out so quickly.She said to the customers standing in front of the counter: Don't worry, everyone, we will definitely increase the supply of small seafood in Laozhi tomorrow.She had already added the seafood market vendor's WeChat account and asked the vendor to deliver more seafood in the afternoon.Hearing Bai Xiangning's promise, customers have raised their expectations again. That's good. Since the supply will be available tomorrow, I will definitely be able to eat it.Well, since Boss Bai has said so, I will come back tomorrow. Let's eat something else today to satisfy our cravings.In the seafood market, a vendor who was sitting on a pony and watching videos on his mobile phone suddenly received a message. The moment he saw the message, he immediately sat up straight and looked at the screen in disbelief.Last time, the customer who added him on WeChat actually ordered hundreds of kilograms of seafood at one time, almost all the seafood varieties here.He quickly contacted his family and asked them to come over to help pack the seafood. For a large order of hundreds of kilograms, he had to take it very seriously and not make any mistakes.Although Bai Xiangning did not come in person this time, the vendors did not dare to fool her with bad seafood. All the seafood they picked were big and lively.He could see that Bai Xiangning was a stable and long-term customer, and he couldn't be too short-sighted. If he offended her for temporary gain, it would be difficult to continue doing business with her later.As long as the quality of the seafood is maintained, people will continue to patronize it.Bai Xiangning ordered seafood for the next day. Since she ordered a large amount this time, it would take a long time to pre-process it. If she didn't order it in advance, it would be too late.The vendor moved very quickly. Less than an hour after Bai Xiangning sent him the message, he drove over. After parking the car in front of the small restaurant, he opened the trunk and let Bai Xiangning Coagulation check.The vendor was very meticulous in his work. Different types of seafood were put in different large buckets. Bai Xiangning fished it out from the bottom with her hands. The seafood she pulled up was as fresh as the one above, so she nodded to the vendor. Said: Okay, please help me carry it to the store, and I will pay you the balance.She had paid the deposit in advance on WeChat.Fang Xin and Qiao Ping also came out to help, and soon moved several large buckets of seafood into the store.Boss Bai, did you buy so many kinds of seafood this time Qiao Ping asked in surprise.Yes, customers like the small seafood in laozhi very much, so I want to add a few more varieties so that customers can have more choices.Fang Xin looked at so many lively seafood in the bucket and said to Bai Xiangning: Boss Bai, do you still plan to let customers choose the type of seafoodBai Xiangning smiled and said: You guessed it rightThis is how I think about it. In addition to the fixed combination of small seafood in the sauce, we can also provide customers with customized services. Generally speaking, they can put whatever seafood they want to eat into the sauce. seafood.Qiao Ping said, "Boss Bai, this is a great idea. In this way, you will definitely attract more customers."Yeah, so we have to get busy. There's so much seafood to deal with.Qiao Ping and Fang Xin immediately rolled up their sleeves and said they were ready to start at any time.At noon the next day, many customers who had not eaten Laozhi seafood the day before came again.Then they were surprised to find a sign on the counter of the small restaurant that read: Fish sauce and small seafood, you can mix and match as you like.Below is the price of each seafood. For example, razor clams are 25 per catty and clams are 15 per catty. The price is calculated by weight.Of course, there are also fixed combinations like yesterday, where there are only four types of seafood, clams, small octopus, prawns and razor clams.One portion is 68 yuan, which is a big bowl, enough for several people.There is also a line at the bottom of the small sign: The freely matched small seafood with sauce needs to be placed in the refrigerator for more than three hours.A customer saw this and asked Bai Xiangning, boss, can't you eat this free combination yetBai Xiangning shook her head, no, it needs to be refrigerated for a few hours to wait for the flavor. If you are in a hurry, you can buy our fixed mix and eat it immediately.After the customer heard this, he immediately became entangled. Another customer queuing behind asked: What if the free-to-order food can be eaten immediatelyHis tone was very serious, but the guests next to him were amused. They said one mouth at a time: It can definitely be eaten, but the taste is probably not that good. Let's see if you are in a hurry to eat it. If you are not in a hurry, Just choose the seafood yourselfBoss, let me have a free mix. I can resist doubts and wait a few hours before eating.Okay, so which ones do you want to chooseThe customer looked at the small brand for a few times, and then said to Bai Xiangning: I want abalone, small octopus, oysters and prawns. Let's have some of the same.Bai Xiangning took a little of each item according to his request. After weighing it on the electronic scale, she said to the customer: A total of 72 yuan.After the customer paid, Bai Xiangning put the selected seafood into the prepared sauce, packaged it and handed it to the customer. It must be refrigerated for a few hours before eating.The customer laughed and said: Don't worry, Boss Bai, I definitely won't eat it right away, I can hold it backAs a result, as soon as he walked out of the small restaurant, he ran to the shade and opened the lid, pinched an abalone from the inside and stuffed it into his mouth.The shell and internal organs of the abalone were removed, and the surface was finely chopped. The meat was very firm and chewy. Although the abalone had just been put into the fish juice, he felt that the taste was not bad at all.At this time, the taste of the juice is very light, with only a thin layer hanging on the surface of the abalone. What you eat in your mouth is more of the original taste of the abalone. After chewing, there is still a hint of sweetness in your mouth.Just when he wanted to eat more, his cell phone rang. It was his wife, so he quickly closed the lid and answered the phone.When will you come back I've been waiting for your little seafood with sauce for a long time.Be back soon, I just came out of the small restaurant.Yesterday, he didn't get the small seafood, and his wife scolded him when he went back, so this time he specially chose the seafood that his wife likes to eat.At this time, another customer in the store said to Bai Xiangning: Boss, I want the same small seafood with fish sauce as yesterday.As one of the twenty lucky people who ate small seafood yesterday, he thought a fixed combination would be good. He couldn't wait a few hours, he wanted to eat it immediately.After returning home with the bag in hand, he took out a can of beer from the refrigerator, sat on the sofa and watched the game.A mouthful of small seafood and a mouthful of beer, even if it is a gout set meal, he is happy with it.The bag also came with disposable gloves. He put on the gloves on his right hand and took out a razor clam. The flesh of the razor clam was covered with dark juice and was crystal clear. He raised his neck slightly and took out the razor clam with its meat and juice. Put them in your mouth together.In order to enhance the customer experience, Bai Xiangning tore off all the yarn from the outer ring of the razor clam meat, so the tender and juicy texture of the razor clam fills your mouth, which is fascinating.He picked up another clam. He only removed the half of the shell without the meat. The meat was not completely peeled out. He always wanted to retain a little self-sufficiency. He sucked the clam with the tip of his tongue, and the tender clam meat slipped in. In the mouth, along with the delicious juice, the whole mouth is occupied by the delicious taste.The customer who chose free matching also arrived home at this time. As soon as he opened the door, his wife rushed to him like a gust of wind. He subconsciously opened his arms. As a result, his wife didn't even look at him and just walked straight to him. He took away the packaging box containing the small seafood from his hand.The wife walked to the dining table, muttering: Let me try the taste of this little seafood in sauce.He remembered what Boss Bai had warned him several times, and quickly said to his wife: Wife, the boss said, this needs to be put in the refrigerator for a few hours before eating.Ah, my wife had already opened the lid, and looked at a large box full of small seafood. She looked confused, but I couldn't help but smell it. It smells so good, and it must taste better.He sat down next to his wife and said solemnly: Listen to me, refrigerate it for a few hours, and the taste will be even better.Is it true His wife looked at him suspiciously, and then said: You didn't even taste a bite when you came back.He denied it flatly. Of course it's gone. I'll definitely have to wait for my wife to eat with you.Really Then why When I just opened it, I could clearly see that the lid was not tightly closed.